I0622478

Ever
After
the collected short works of
Marie Sexton

Ever After

Editing by Sue Laybourn
Cover art by A.J. Corza
Formatting by Kelly Smith
http://mariesexton.net

Published by Marie Sexton, 2015
ISBN: 978-0-9961741-0-7

Trademarks Acknowledgement

The author acknowledges the trademarked status and trademark owners of the following wordmarks mentioned in these works of fiction:

Cheez Whiz: Kraft Foods Group, Inc
Just For Men: Combe Incorporated
Jeep Wrangler: FCA US LLC
Facebook: Facebook, Inc
Subaru Outback: Fuji Heavy Industries
Tevas: Deckers Outdoor Corporation
Miracle on 34th Street: 20th Century Fox
Left Hand Brewery: Left Hand Brewing Company

Contents

To Feel the Sun

The sun is high and bold in the Colorado sky, baking the grass beneath my feet, turning the world hot and dry. Above me, the heavens are bluer than a robin's egg, unmarred by even a wisp of white.

I shouldn't be cold, but I am. I can't stop shivering.

I hear the gurgle of the river, still out of sight over the ridge. Other than that, it's silent. The birds were singing this morning, but now they've grown quiet. The thick stillness of the autumn day is beginning. The only thing stirring is a rattlesnake, somewhere deep in the grass. I hear him: rattling, then being still, rattling, then being still. My feet move in time with him, as if dancing to his tune. Rattle-step-step, silence-step-step, rattle-step-step, silence-step-step.

There's something unnatural about it, and it's this recognition that brings me up short. I turn to look behind me, toward my grandfather's big farmhouse. From here, I shouldn't be able to see it. It should be blocked by trees and distance, and yet it's there, larger than life.

This is a dream. It's not August. Not anymore. It's early December, unless I've been sick longer than I thought. Not even twenty years old, and yet I may not see my next birthday. Somewhere inside that house, I am lying, racked with illness. If I concentrate, I can feel the way my body shakes from the fever. I can feel the weight of the quilts that can't warm me.

The dream is better, and so I turn away from the house, back toward the bright August day. I know where I'm going — where I always go. To the gently sloping bank above the river, the large, flat, sun-drenched rocks that overlook the water, and the tree that bears our initials.

I'm going to see Teddy.

I shiver and wrap my arms around myself, hoping the sun will warm me soon. It should. I can tell it's going to be one hell of a hot day. The ground is practically steaming. Later, the clouds will roll in from the west. The molten blue sky will sizzle with anticipation, the heat will crackle and break, and then the rain will come, cool and fresh, quenching the ground and cooling the earth. Only fifteen or twenty minutes — thirty at the most — then the storm will move off, leaving the grass damp and pungent, as if all of nature has breathed a sigh of relief. I know this because I've seen it happen over and over again, the cycle of front-range weather that's often as predictable as the sun. As predictable as the start and stop of the snake's strangely rhythmic rattle.

His sound is a warning, but he's no threat to me.

I find the tree and lie back in the grass, not quite in the shade. I need to feel the sun. Teddy isn't here yet, but he will be. This is our spot. The only place we've ever had privacy. The place we played as children, splashing in the shallow water. The place we came as teenagers to smoke cigarettes stolen from his father, or to taste the gin stolen from mine. It's the place we first touched. And kissed.

The place we fell in love.

I remember him lying by my side, back when our innocent friendship was just turning into something new and exhilarating. That hadn't been in August. That had been in May, 1917, more than a year ago. We were lying on the bank, in this exact spot. Side by side, and yet a bit too close to each other. I was hyperaware of his breathing. Of the rise and fall of his chest, just visible in my peripheral vision. And then he touched my hand.

He didn't hold it. Instead, he caressed me. He brushed his fingertip over the sensitive flesh between my thumb and first finger. It was so simple, but the heart-poundingly erotic joy of it sent shivers up my spine. I closed my eyes and concentrated on his touch — down and over the base of my thumb, around the curve of my wrist and back up, along the back of my hand to my knuckles, then a slow, steady tickle to the tip of my finger.

Back on that distant day, the sun had warmed my eyelids. My chest. My groin. I had drawn a deep, shaky breath, suddenly aware that I'd become unabashedly aroused. I was torn about how to react. Surely, I'd thought, I should pull away. I should make a joke. Run to the cold water of the river and turn this all back into a game.

But I didn't want that, and somehow I knew Teddy didn't either. So I remained motionless as he slid his fingers into my palm. He circled the tender skin there, making me whimper. He caressed my fingers, one at a time, stroking them from knuckle to tip, as if it were some more intimate part of me he was touching, and the slow tease of it made me yearn for exactly that. It was as if each nerve was more sensitive than it had ever been before. As if each sensation on my hand could be felt everywhere — my arm, my stomach, the back of my neck, and best of all, in the deep, pulsing ache of my groin. I had never felt that way. I'd touched myself, brought myself to fruition, but even that hadn't compared to the feel of Teddy's fingers on mine.

My heart pounded and my breath came in trembling, labored pants. His fingers moved away, and I nearly moaned in disappointment, but then I felt him above me. I opened my eyes. He had rolled toward me, nearly on top of me, propping himself on his elbow. His cheeks were red, his lips moist.

He asked, in a whisper, "Can I kiss you?"

I nodded, unable to speak.

He moved slowly. Whether he was afraid I'd pull away, or afraid I wouldn't, I didn't know, but I lay still until his trembling lips met mine.

Even now, in my dream inside a dream, I can't quite remember the details, but I remember the sensations. The breathless urgency as we grew bolder. The unbuttoned pants and exploring hands. The way he panted in my ear as we stroked and strained. The way it was over far too quickly and we'd lain there, not minding the sticky mess between us, staring into each other's eyes.

"Can we do it again?" he'd asked.

And we had. We'd spent a blissful summer meeting whenever we could, falling frantically into each other's arms, learning just how deep and amazing our passion could be.

But then summer had ended, and I'd had to leave my grandfather's farm as I did every fall. I had to go back to town, back to my mother's house, in time for the start of school. It was my first year at the university.

And Teddy, for some reason I'd never quite understood, had enlisted.

The truth comes back to me then, like a knife in my throat, and there, in my dream construct of that place — the place where Teddy and I had fished and played as kids, the place where we'd made love as young adults — I curl into a ball and cry.

Teddy is dead, killed somewhere in France. I don't know the details — only saw his name on that horrible, dreaded list in the paper — but the memory of his death comes with an image of his body, broken and bloody, lying forgotten in some Godforsaken trench. It's a construct of my imagination and nothing more, and yet it's haunted me for months. The war may be over, but peace won't bring Teddy back.

The last day we had together was a day like this one — the bright, vibrant heat of August scorching the earth, the Colorado sun beating down on us as we struggled to say goodbye. We should have spent the day loving each other, finding what pleasure we could, but we'd fought instead. He'd begged me to enlist with him. I thought he'd gone mad. And so our summer of discovery had ended in a bitter, mournful silence.

I've been lost ever since.

The thought of him always brings the heartbreak back, but I don't have the strength to cry for long. My tears slow, and I lie there in the grass, exhausted, listening to wind. Somewhere to my right, the rattlesnake continues his unnaturally patterned racket.

"Benjamin."

It's Teddy, here at last. I sit up, rubbing the tears from my eyes. For half a second, I worry he'll be like that image in my mind, his uniform soaked with blood, the pallor of death upon his skin, but when I look, I find him the way he was in that last perfect summer — fit and healthy, his cheeks bronzed by the sun, his hair blowing across his face. He's dressed in the same simple work clothes he always wore, and the familiarity of the moment makes my heart ache.

"Hello," I say. The horrible inadequacy of the word is like a weight in my chest.

Teddy leans against the tree and smiles at me. "Hello back."

A dream. All a dream. Teddy is dead, and I'm in a fever-induced delirium. I remember the epidemic sweeping through the town, and the paper reporting alarming death tolls from all over the state. I remember deciding, along with my mother, to flee to the country and the perceived safety of the fresh air of my grandfather's farm. But it was too late. I was already sick.

Yes, this sun-drenched August afternoon is a figment of my imagination, but I don't care. I don't want reality — the dark, oppressive room, reeking of illness, the pain that sinks bone-deep, the labored breathing. I only want to stay with Teddy. "Are you really here?"

He laughs. "Can't you see me?"

"Yes, but…"

"I didn't mean to make you wait, but I hadn't expect you to be here so soon."

"You're dead."

He shrugs, as if it's a moot point. As if I've said nothing more than, "your hair is brown," or "your eyes are hazel." His expression is sheepishly amused. "I suppose you made the right decision, not enlisting."

I find no humor in the situation. Only pain and grief. "Why wouldn't you listen to me?" I ask, standing to face him. "Why wouldn't you stay?"

"For what, Ben? To spend my whole life working my daddy's farm, waiting every year for the three short months you're here before going back to your real life? Waiting for the day you'd come back only to tell me you'd found a wife?" His voice cracks, and I know he's fighting tears. "Waiting for the year when you didn't come at all?"

My eyes sting and my throat is tight, but he isn't crying, so neither will I. "You could have moved to town with me."

He turns away, not needing to answer. It's a repeat of the argument we had on that fateful last day. I know why he refused my suggestion. We couldn't have been lovers in town. It would have meant sneaking around, hiding ourselves, telling lies.

But at least he would still be alive.

The dry grass crunches beneath my feet as I cross to him. I touch the place where we once carved our initials into the tree. "The day we did this, we said 'forever.' I meant that."

"So did I."

I sigh, because there's no answer now, just as there wasn't one then. The world wasn't made for men like us. "I loved you, Teddy. God, I loved you so much."

He nods, and I see the pain of that last day in his eyes. "I loved you too. I still do."

"That summer... Those were the best months of my life."

"Mine too."

"If only we could have made time stand still."

"Now we can."

I'm not sure what he means, but I don't care. I hold my hand out to him. "We can be together? Like before."

He smiles at me and a slow blush creeps its way up his cheeks. "Soon."

He reaches to take my hand, but it slips through mine. I can't touch him and the realization makes me want to cry again. It seems unfair. Everything else here is so real. The ground is solid. The tree is strong and rigid next to me, the bark rough and unyielding. And yet Teddy is beyond my reach.

"Soon," he says again, moving closer.

I can feel him now, and yet not in the way I'd like. He isn't flesh and blood, but he's warm. More than that. He is warmth itself. Warmer than the sun. For the first time since falling sick, I don't feel cold. I stop shivering. I let him wrap me up in his radiance. I fall blissfully into his heat. I remember with blinding clarity the feeling of flesh on flesh, the whisper of our skin, the taste of his kiss.

"Be with me," he says.

I close my eyes and I let myself drift as he teases me to passion. No, I can't quite feel the touch of his hands or the brush of his lips, but I remember. I *know*. I sense him with me, our thoughts mingling as our bodies merge. Soon I'm gasping, panting, straining, climaxing like I haven't in ages. Not since that summer.

Not since him.

"You haven't changed," he says, sounding amused. "I love the sounds you make."

"I wish I could feel you."

"Soon."

"You keep saying that."

"Because it's true."

"I'll get to touch you?"

"Yes."

"And kiss you?"

"I promise."

"Will that be a dream too?"

He laughs, although it's a sound of mirth more than joy. He steps back, away from me, and the chill of the fever immediately returns, worse than ever. My bones seem to rattle with the force of my trembling. "Don't you understand? I'm here to show you the way."

"The way?" And then, almost as soon as I say the words, I grasp his meaning. "I'm dying."

He nods slowly, watching me carefully, judging my reaction. "Can't you feel it?"

Can I? I feel the fever, yes, but nothing more. Not from here. To do that, I'll have to reach back to my real place in the world, and yet that will mean leaving him.

"Go ahead," he says gently, as if sensing my dilemma. "I'll wait."

I wish I could hold his hand, just to be sure I don't lose him again, but I can't. Instead, I hang onto the tree. I anchor myself on our initials, carved more than a year ago into the deep, gray bark, and I focus my gaze inward. I concentrate on the feeling of my body. The shivering. The aches.

The rattle.

It's not a snake.

It's me. It's the sounds of my breathing. Each breath comes harder than the one before. I'm losing the strength to push air past the fluid that fills my lungs. I'm not sure when the pneumonia set in, but I know without doubt that's what it is.

I really am going to die.

Perhaps I should panic, but I don't. I'm relieved. All those months without Teddy. The knowledge of our argument and his death. The pain of knowing I'd never be able to love any-body the way I'd loved him. It's been so hard to fight the sickness when I have no reason to live.

I open my eyes again to face him. "What happens now?"

"All you have to do is follow me."

And I do. Over the parched ground, across the river, through the lands of our youth. The cold falls away. My shivering subsides. He reaches out to take my hand and as we walk, his fingers grow solid against mine. I find myself smiling. I'm warm at last.

I've never been so happy to feel the sun.

Chapter Five and the
Axe-Wielding Maniac

I was rewriting the first paragraph of chapter five for at least the eight-hundredth time when the axe-wielding maniac knocked on my front door.

And yes, since you asked, of course it was a Monday.

Okay, truth be told, eight-hundred might be a bit of an exaggeration. It was closer to thirty. And it wasn't actually an axe. It was a pickaxe. Here's the thing though: a strapping young man strolling through the Oregon woods on a sunny August morning might have put a regular axe to industrious use. A pickaxe, on the other hand? Only a homicidal maniac needed one of those. He carried it slung over his right shoulder, Paul Bunyan-style, and if I needed any more evidence of his foul intentions, I found it in his left hand: a crowbar.

I stood in the cool near-dark inside my cabin, squinting through the peep-hole into the bright sunny day, wondering what exactly I should do. Turning around and going right back to bed seemed like my best bet.

"Hello?" the maniac called as he reached out to bang on the door with the curved end of the crowbar. "Good morning!"

It seemed he wasn't planning on going away, and while normally I'd be thrilled to have a handsome young man practically beating down my front door, I felt sure this one was going to cause me trouble. He bounced excitedly on the balls of his toes, grinning ear to ear. I wondered if all murderous psychos were so cheery when they knocked on their victim's doors. Then again, I had to wonder how many psychos bothered to knock at all. It was a fact I might look up later, assuming I lived through the morning.

"Who are you and what do you want?" I yelled through the door.

His excitement seemed to kick into overdrive at the sound of my voice. He bounced a little faster on his feet, and his eyes were bright. "Mr. Hill? Is that you? My name is Redd Foxx, sir, and I just need a few moments of your time."

Redd Foxx? Did he actually expect me to believe that? Then again, had I actually expected a pick axe-wielding lunatic to give me his real name?

I cracked the door open half an inch and eyed him through the gap. Mid-twenties, fit and tan and trim. He had dark blond hair that didn't appear to have been combed in weeks. He wore tan cargo shorts and a faded Orange Crush T-shirt. And on his feet were hiking boots and wool socks, even though it had to be over seventy-five degrees outside.

Even I had to admit, he didn't exactly *look* like a serial killer. Then again, wasn't that what everybody said after the police found body parts and human fingernails in the ice cream tub in some nutjob's freezer?

"Really sir," he said, "if you'll just give me a few minutes, I think you'll be interested in what I have to say."

I debated for a moment, but in the end, my curiosity won out. Maybe he'd kill me and maybe he wouldn't. Either way, it wasn't like I'd been making progress on chapter five to begin with. I opened the door.

He stopped bouncing, and his jaw dropped a bit. "Joshua Hill?" he asked, suddenly sounding a bit unsure.

"Yes."

"Joshua Franklin Hill, the writer?"

"*Yes*," I said again. "Were you expecting somebody else?"

"Well, no. It's just, you know, you look a lot younger in that picture on the back of your books."

I stopped short of slamming the door in his face. My age was a bit of a touchy subject for me. I'd only just turned forty-two, but I knew I appeared older. The fact that my lover of eight years had recently left me for a twenty-four year old didn't help matters.

The man must have recognized my annoyance because he suddenly started bouncing on his feet again, and he rushed forward, his words tumbling out in a rush. "Mr. Hill, I'm such a big fan. Really. You have no idea how excited I was when I found out you were the one who lived here. I mean, what a coincidence, right? It's so great to meet you."

"What do you want?"

"Well, sir," he said as if it were the most normal thing in the world, "I'd like to dig up your living room floor."

This time, I really did slam the door in his face. My first assumption had been correct: he *was* a maniac. Maybe not homicidal, but still a bit off his rocker. Batshit. Loopy. Whack-a-doo.

Plus, he'd practically called me old.

"Mr. Hill," he called, "I've come all the way from Moab, Utah to talk to you."

"You should have tried email!"

"Have you ever heard the name Alton Fox?"

"Not that I recall."

"Mr. Hill, please!"

I opened the door again and leaned against its edge with my arms crossed. He took a deep breath, and I knew he was about to launch into some long-winded explanation. "Look," I said, cutting him off before he could start, "I'm really busy at the moment." Really busy getting absolutely fucking nowhere on the book I'd been trying to write for five months now, but I didn't feel compelled to share details. "Do me a favor and cut to the chase."

He stopped short, and some of the wind went out of his sails. He considered for a moment, then said, "I have reason to believe there's something of value hidden under the floorboards of your cabin."

"'Something of value'?" I asked skeptically. "Pirate gold?"

I meant it as a joke, but he didn't seem to realize it. "Alton wasn't a pirate."

"It doesn't matter. You're not digging up my floor."

He actually had the nerve to look surprised, as if it had never occurred to him that showing up on somebody's front porch with a pick-axe and a crowbar and asking to destroy their home was a perfectly reasonable request.

"Sir, I think if you'd let me explain — "

"Listen, Redd — "

"*Rad.*"

"What?"

"My name's Rad."

I sighed, rubbing my forehead in an effort to fend off the headache I was sure was imminent. Why me? Why now? Why hadn't I listened to my mother and become a doctor? Or a lawyer? Or a teacher? Or a panhandler back in San Diego? Why had I even bothered to get up today? What a perfectly good waste of coffee it had turned out to be so far.

"You really expect me to believe that your mother named you 'Rad'?"

"Well, it's Radcliffe, technically. Radcliffe Fox."

"Okay, Cliff — "

"It's *Rad*!"

"Whatever. The point is, there's absolutely no way I'm allowing you to dig up my living room floor."

"But — "

"Now, if you'll excuse me, I have a book to write."

I didn't bother listening to his protests. I closed the door.

And I went straight back to bed.

If there's one thing I should have learned from cable TV, it's that weapon-wielding nutjobs don't go away when you close the door. Michael Myers, Jason Voorhees, Freddy Krueger — even that stupid demon-possessed doll — no matter what you do, they just keep coming back. Usually, with a better weapon.

Rad's better weapon was coconut chicken curry.

I could smell it as soon as I opened the door. I'd sequestered myself in my cabin in an effort to force myself to write, telling myself I could venture out again once I'd completed chapter five. As a result, I'd been living on frozen pizzas and Cheez Whiz sandwiches for the last four days. The idea of real food made my mouth water.

"Hungry?" he asked, holding up a large paper bag from Tai's Thai. In his other hand was a six-pack of beer. Not crap beer, either, but one from a local micro-brewery.

They say the way to a man's heart is through his stomach. My heart felt completely unaffected, but I did find myself opening my front door.

He followed me into the kitchen. My tiny table was covered with cups and glasses, plus my notes and laptop. I pushed them aside to make room for us to eat.

"Working on the latest adventures of Alex Daring?"

"Trying to," I admitted as I gathered up ancient coffee cups and carried them to the sink. "It's slow going."

"I've read the first eight books. I was wondering when the next one would come out."

"So's my editor." My treasure-seeking character had garnered me a healthy income over the years, but the demand for one more book had long since become tiresome.

"The cabin's bigger than I expected. Did somebody add on?"

"My father." The cabin had initially been only two rooms. My father had added electricity, and expanded the small kitchen. He'd also insulated the windows and added a hearth that ran the length of the tiny living room. Still, the only heat came from the fireplace. The floor was nothing but wooden planks over a dirt foundation. My father had used it as a fishing cabin. I now used it as writing refuge a few months out of the year. The rest of the time, it sat empty.

"Mr. Hill," Rad said as I sat down, "I realize I probably came on a bit strong this morning—"

"Is there a subtle way to ask to tear up a man's floor?"

He smiled apologetically. "I suppose not."

I dug enthusiastically into the curry. It was spicy enough to make me sweat. Rad glanced around my small cabin with unabashed curiosity, which gave me a chance to study him. My impression was much as it had been that morning:

twenties, fit, an outdoorsy type. I noticed one thing though I hadn't seen earlier: a braided rainbow bracelet around his right wrist. I'd be lying if I said I wasn't suddenly a lot more willing to hear him out.

"Okay." I leaned back and opened a second beer. "Let's hear it."

He'd obviously been waiting to be given the green light. "How much do you know about the history of this cabin?"

"I know that it was built by my great uncle, Winston Hill. He killed himself a couple of years later, and it passed to his younger brother."

"Your grandfather?"

"Yes."

"Do you know why Winston killed himself?"

The question surprised me. "No. It happened long before I was born." By the time I'd been old enough to be curious, my grandfather had passed away. "My father said my grandfather never liked to talk about it."

Rad winced. "I'm sure." He drained his beer and reached for a second one. "And you've never heard of Alton Fox?"

"Should I have?"

"Mr. Hill—"

"My name's Josh."

"Josh," he conceded with a smile, before continuing. "Alton Fox is my grandfather, and he helped Winston build this cabin. He says he and Winston had saved all of their money, and that it's buried here."

"Where, exactly?"

He stood, and I followed him into the living room. He pointed to the northeast corner of the room, by the fireplace. "Right here."

I wasn't sure what to say. I still didn't want to let him dig up my floor. That much was certain.

Rad got down on his hands and knees and began crawling around, apparently testing for loose boards.

"Why now?" I asked. "If the money's been here all this time, why does your grandfather suddenly need it?"

He didn't look at me. He kept crawling around the floor, testing boards. "Honestly, I don't think it's about the money so much as about making peace with what happened." He leaned down and tried to peer through a crack between two of the floorboards.

"I see," I said.

I certainly was seeing something, but it had nothing to do with his grandfather and my great uncle, and everything in the world to do with a strapping young man on his hands and knees in front of me, his ass sticking in the air, pointing my direction like an invitation.

"He carried this secret his whole life," he went on, apparently unaware of my suddenly lecherous thoughts. "I think he needed somebody to confess it to."

"And that somebody was you?"

"Well, I guess I was the logical answer, once he realized—" He stopped short, and I pulled my eyes away from his backside to find him grinning at me over his shoulder. "Are you checking me out?"

My cheeks burned. I was suddenly glad I hadn't shaved in a few days, because it would make it harder for him to see my blush. "No!"

His grin grew, and I knew I wasn't fooling him at all. He shook his ass at me, and I chose to stare at the ceiling rather than let myself be distracted by it. He laughed, which annoyed me. I made myself meet his eyes. He was still on the floor, but he was sitting up now, smiling at me.

"So, you still want to dig up my floor?" I asked.

"You want to have sex?"

"*What?*"

He shrugged. "Just a question."

"Jesus! I don't even know you!"

"So?"

I had absolutely no idea what to say. Did I want to have sex? Of course I did. I'm male, after all, and I hadn't had sex with anybody since Roger had left me. But did I want to have sex with Rad? *That* was the question. He was certainly attractive, but I'd never been one for casual pickups. They made me unbelievably self-conscious. "I…um…" That was as much as I managed to say.

He stood up and brushed his knees off. He shook his head. "Your generation is so uptight about sex."

My generation?

"How old do you think I am?"

"Listen, it's getting late. I should go."

"I thought you wanted to dig up my floor!" As soon as I said it, I realized I sounded defensive. I also began to wonder if "dig up my floor" sounded like a euphemism for something else entirely, and I felt myself blushing again.

"Did you change your mind about letting me?"

"No."

"Did you change your mind about the sex?"

"No!"

"Well then, not much reason to stay." He turned to leave, but stopped in my door and glanced at me over his shoulder. "I'm staying at that Lamplight Motel on Main Street. I'll be here a couple more days." He smiled at me. "Give me a call if you change your mind."

It wasn't until after he left that I stopped to wonder if he was talking about the floor or the sex.

I stood in the bathroom the next morning regarding myself in the mirror. Rad's reference to my age still bugged me. Sure, I was older than him, and unlike *his* parents, mine had given me a sensible name, rather than one that implied a fifteen-year old skateboarder, but I was still only forty-two.

And sure, Roger had left me for a younger man, but the truth was, our relationship had been on the rocks for years. It wasn't that we fought. It was just that we no longer had anything to say to each other. I hadn't been at all surprised when he'd moved out. Still, it had hurt when I'd found out he was already living with another man only a few weeks later. The fact that his new boyfriend was eighteen years younger than me and an aerobics instructor to boot certainly hadn't done much for my ego.

Still, I wasn't old.

Not old at all.

That's what I tried to tell myself, but the truth was, I'd let myself go a bit in the weeks I'd been at the cabin. I needed a haircut. I hadn't shaved in ages. My beard was more gray than brown. There was gray at my temples, too.

I sighed. Too bad nobody had given me advance warning about the axe-wielding maniac. I might have made myself a bit more presentable.

I shaved my traitorous beard and made myself go for a run for the first time in weeks. Afterward, I showered and headed into town for some groceries. I hadn't finished chapter five, but I'd proven that denying myself real meals wasn't going to get the book done any sooner.

I loaded the cart with bread and sandwich meat, chips and soda, and a few Hungry Man frozen dinners. I should have left then, but instead, I found myself in the hair care aisle, staring blankly at a shelf of Just For Men. Would I look younger if I used it?

Don't be stupid. Just walk away.

After all, hair dye was like makeup and pantyhose — it was for women. Except this, of course, which was for men.

Just For Men.

I sighed. Was it so bad being grey? Did it mean that much to me to appear younger? Was I truly so vain?

I thought about Roger and his new boyfriend.

I thought about Rad saying, "Your generation is so uptight about sex."

Yes, I decided at that moment. I really was that vain.

I eyed the boxes again. There was a surprisingly large selection of colors. Was I a Light Medium-Brown, or a Medium Brown, or a Medium-Dark Brown? There was also a plain old Dark Brown. I foolishly searched the aisle for a mirror so I could try to compare the hair on my head to that on the box. No such luck. Not Darkest Brown. I could rule that out, as well as the blonds and the blacks.

I picked up the box of Medium Brown and began to read the directions.

"Hey Josh!"

I glanced up and felt the blood drain from my face. Rad was advancing down the aisle toward me, carrying a hand-held basket in one hand, his other hand raised in greeting. I quickly tried to shove the box back onto the shelf, but it wobbled and fell to the floor. I pushed my cart forward to meet him, hoping he'd assume I was shopping for shampoo. "Hello," I said.

"You shaved off your beard!"

"Oh." I put my hand up and stupidly felt my cheek, as if I hadn't realized. "It was getting itchy." And gray.

That made me think of the hair dye. A quick glance at the floor showed that it was right next to my foot.

"Listen, I don't go back to Utah until tomorrow, and I don't know anybody but you. How do you feel about dinner?"

"Dinner?" I tried to casually kick the box under my cart, but it hit the wheel instead and bounced back toward me. Rad was watching me, and I made myself hold still. "Uhm. Sure. Okay." I pushed the box sideways with my foot, shoving it under the overhang of the bottom shelf. I breathed a mental sigh of relief that it was out of sight. "Where?"

"This is your town. You tell me."

"There's an Italian place on Main, just down from your motel."

"Sounds great! Five o'clock?"

"Five?"

"Yeah. I know older people like to eat early."

"I'm not that old, you know!"

"No offense, man. It's cool. I'll see you then."

He started to walk past me, but suddenly he stopped. He leaned over and reached behind me, under the shelf to retrieve the box of hair dye. I felt my cheeks turn bright red. Was there any point in pretending it wasn't mine?

He put it back in the empty space on the shelf, then turned to me with a smile. "I like the gray."

He left me standing there feeling completely embarrassed. And a little silly. And a little bit flattered, too.

⌒⬭⬭⌒

I arrived at the restaurant that evening with my gray hair intact.

Rad was dressed much as before, except he'd traded his cargo shorts for jeans. They did very little to dress up the faded Cat in the Hat T-shirt he was wearing. I'd been thinking of the dinner as a date, but upon seeing his casual dress, I was suddenly unsure. I'd spent a stupid amount of time debating my own wardrobe before leaving the house. I was glad I'd opted against the tie.

We sipped beers while we waited for our food to arrive. I was a bit uncomfortable, but he seemed completely at ease.

"You don't actually live here in Oregon, do you?" he asked.

"No. I live in San Diego. I come up here when I need a change of scenery."

"For writing, you mean?"

Yes, or when I just wanted to get away from the memories of my failed relationship. "I have a deadline looming. I hoped coming up here would help clear my head."

"And is it working?"

"Not as well as I'd hoped."

"Well, it isn't actually a change of scenery, is it? I mean, the cabin's been in your family forever. You've stayed up here before. Maybe you need to go someplace completely new. Find an adventure!"

"An adventure?"

"Yeah. Your stories are about adventure. Maybe you need one of your own."

"Like digging up lost treasure?"

He laughed. "Sure. Why not?"

It was certainly true that my life was about as far from an adventure as one could get. I'd been stuck in ruts for years, both in my relationship with Roger, and in my writing. "What do you do?" I asked him.

He fidgeted with the salt shaker rather than meet my gaze. "Well, I majored in philosophy."

The way he said it was self-deprecating, and it made me laugh. "So you're unemployed?"

"Not quite," he said, smiling. "Moab's a tourist spot, especially during the summer. I do Jeep tours, and I work as a rafting guide on occasion. When the tourists aren't around, I do odd jobs for people. Or I wait tables for a few weeks until there's something else to do."

My first thought was that it seemed like a very unreliable source of income. My second thought was that I really was getting old. "That does sound like a bit of an adventure."

Our food arrived, and we fell silent as we ate. I found myself comparing his lifestyle to my own. I was a homebody, and I lived comfortably. I made good money from my books and I should have been happy, but the truth was, the fun of being a writer had long since waned. I'd come to think of it as a chore more than a hobby. It had been a very long time since I'd woken up in the morning with any kind of enthusiasm for my day.

It was a downright depressing realization.

"Tell me about Winston and your grandfather," I said in order to distract myself.

He set his fork down and put his elbows on the table, leaning closer with a knowing grin. "They were lovers."

That surprised me. I hadn't realized my great uncle was gay. Then again, I'd never known the man, so how I would have known? "And they built the cabin together?"

"It was their love shack," he said, waggling his eyebrows suggestively.

I shuddered. "I'd rather not think about it."

He laughed. "That's only because you're thinking of them as old men, but they were in their early twenties at the time."

He was right of course. For some reason, I'd been thinking of them at the age my grandfather had been at his death.

"They were young and crazy in love, and they'd go up to that cabin to be together."

"So what happened?"

He picked his fork up again and started to push what was left of his meal around on his plate. "My grandpa likes to remind me how much easier it is for us these days. He likes to make sure I know how much harder it was back then. The thing is, I think he feels guilty."

"About what?"

"Well, Winston wanted them to be together. That's why they were saving up their money. Winston thought they could move somewhere where nobody knew them—

"Where?"

"Well, that was one of the points of contention."

"'One of?'"

"My grandfather couldn't stand the thought of his family finding out about him. I think he assumed all along that he and Winston would each marry nice girls and settle down, and keep their relationship on the down-low. But Winston started pushing for them to leave, and Alton panicked."

"He broke things off?"

"Yes. And even worse, he got engaged."

"That's why Winston killed himself?"

Rad shrugged without meeting my eyes. "According to my grandfather, yes." He shook his head. "It's a tough thing. He says he can't completely regret what he did, because he loves his family. He wouldn't go back and give up having kids. But at the same time, I think he loved Winston. I *know* he loved Winston. Probably far more than he ever loved my grandmother. I think he hoped Winston would come to accept the marriage and take him back. That they could go back to having the cabin as their hideaway."

"But Winston killed himself instead."

Rad nodded. "Alton never expected that."

"And the money?"

"They had it hidden up at the cabin. Alton never wanted to try to claim it, because he was afraid of having to explain things to Winston's family. And I don't think he felt like he deserved it."

"But now he wants it?"

"Like I said, I don't think it's about the money. I think he's hoping there are other things with the money."

"Like what?"

"A pocket watch, for one. Winston had given it to Alton, and Alton gave it back when he broke things off. After Winston died, Alton never knew what happened to it. He's hoping it's there, with the money." He put his fork down. He wiped his face with his napkin, and slowly drained his beer. I had the feeling he was collecting his thoughts, trying to decide what more there was to say. "My grandfather bears a lot of guilt over what happened. I think it's easy for us to judge, but things were different then. Anyway, now that he's nearing the end, I think he longs for some kind of closure."

The waiter came to clear our plates and offer dessert, which we declined. Rad and I sat in silence while I thought about what he'd told me. He was right. It was easy to blame Alton for Winston's death, but how much different had things been back then?

I glanced around the restaurant. I saw families, and other couples. No other same-sex couples, and yet we were here, dining together in the open. Nobody seemed to have noticed, let alone mind. I knew without a doubt I could have reached across the table and taken his hand, and nobody would have done much more than blink. And yet for Winston and Alton, every word must have felt risky, every glance dangerous. Over the years, I'd encountered bigots and discrimination, but those incidents were the exception to an otherwise unobstructed life. I learned to avoid the bank teller who sneered at me, and the snickers of passing fools, but could I have dealt with an entire town? Could I have faced cutting all ties with my family in order to run off with my secret lover, not knowing if or where we'd ever find acceptance?

I looked up to find Rad watching me. For once, he wasn't smiling. He was somber.

"I'll let you dig up my floor, but dinner's on you."

His face broke into a broad, slow smile. "Deal."

Rad followed me in his rental car back to my cabin. The drive took several minutes. I found myself fidgety. My heart beat a bit faster than usual. My stomach was strangely unsettled. I drummed impatiently on the steering wheel when I had to stop at one of the town's few stoplights. It was something I hadn't felt in so long, it actually took me a minute to pinpoint the emotion.

I was excited.

It seemed strange to admit, but it was true. The idea of digging up my living room floor had piqued my interest. It wasn't even the idea of what we might find so much as the idea of doing something new. Something completely outside my norm.

Once at the cabin, I helped Rad carry in his tools — a crowbar, a shovel, and the pickaxe that had first alerted me to his insanity. Did I still think he was loony? Yes. Undoubtedly so. But I was also beginning to think I could use a bit of insanity in my life.

"What should I do?" I asked him when we got inside.

"I'll do the work," he said. "It's only fair. Besides, it's easier for somebody my age."

"I'm not that old, you know."

He stepped closer and put his hand on my forearm. He was shorter than me, but not by much. He smiled up at me flirtatiously. "It's okay. I like older men."

"I'm not 'older'."

"You're older than me."

My first instinct was to argue that being older than him didn't make me old, but what was the point? He was flirting with me. He liked me. My age suddenly seemed far less important. "Fine," I said instead. "You dig. I'll drink."

I pulled a beer out of the fridge and went into the living room to watch him work. I couldn't quite make myself sit down and relax, though. I was anxious and impatient. Excited and nervous. I was, I began to realize, horny as hell. I watched Rad — the way his biceps bulged as he worked, the muscles of his back rippling under his shirt, his ass firm and muscular as he pulled up the boards in the corner of the room. His hair was messy, his cheeks stubbly, his hands strong and calloused. He was young and dynamic, mysterious and yet somehow simple and unassuming. He was like a spring breeze, waking me from a long, tedious hibernation.

Rad finally finished moving floorboards. The two-by-fours that held the floorboards were still there, but the dirt foundation was visible half a foot underneath them. The hole in he'd made was roughly three feet by three feet, right against the hearth in the northeast corner of the room.

"Huh," Rad said as he stared down through it to the dirt lying a few inches below. "That's odd."

"What?" I asked. I didn't see anything unexpected. Just smooth packed dirt.

"I thought it would be right here. I mean, he said it was buried, but only barely. I thought the spot would be obvious."

"Well, it's been nearly sixty years."

"I suppose," he said, but he didn't sound convinced.

He stepped down into the hole. There wasn't room for him to use the pickaxe effectively, so I handed him the shovel, and he started to dig. He started in the northeast corner. He dug down about ten inches, but there was no sign of Alton and Winston's stash.

"It shouldn't be any deeper than this," he said.

"Maybe it's not exactly in the corner?"

He continued to dig, expanding his excavation further into the opening until he'd overturned every inch of dirt in the space. He found nothing.

"I don't understand," he said, looking up at me. "It should be here."

I had no idea what to tell him. "Maybe it's in the other corner?"

"He said the northeast corner."

"It was a long time ago. Maybe he was confused."

He smiled at me. "Are you offering to let me dig up even more of your floor?"

Was I? "Maybe."

I held my hand down to him and helped him step out of the hole. His hand was rough. The hair of his forearms was smeared with dirt. When he stepped up next to me, I could smell him. He smelled like soap and sweat and clean, overturned earth. It was sexy as hell.

"I'm really sorry, Josh. It should have been here. I did all this damage for nothing."

"No," I said. "It wasn't for nothing." Because for the first time in ages, I felt inspired. I felt alive and awake. I felt *young*.

I realized I was still holding his hand. He stared at me, smiling a bit. A patch of faded freckles were sprinkled across his nose. He had full lips. A strong jaw. A neck that I suddenly wanted very much to kiss. I wondered if his chest was smooth or hairy. I felt desperate in a way I hadn't in years.

"Josh?" he asked.

"Yes?"

"You want to have sex now?"

"I thought you'd never ask!"

The next thing I knew, he was all over me. We couldn't seem to get our clothes off fast enough.

I wouldn't ever have said that sex with Roger had been bad — how bad could sex really be, after all? — but in the last few years of our relationship, it had definitely lost its edge. It had become mechanical. Almost impersonal. Sex by rote. Something we did more out of habit than out of desire.

This was exactly the opposite. There was a playful franticness to it that made my pulse race. It made my body thrum. I was torn between wanting to explore every inch of him and wanting to simply fuck his brains out.

"Oh Jesus," I panted, suddenly bringing myself up short as I fought to unbutton his pants. "I don't have any condoms!"

He laughed and reached into his back pocket. He pulled out one of the square foil packages and held it up for me to see.

"You brought one with you?"

"I brought five."

"*Five?*"

He shrugged, smiling as he pulled me in for a kiss. "I had high hopes for the night."

"You think an old guy like me has that kind of stamina?"

He smiled and kissed me again. "You're not that old."

"Damn right, I'm not."

It was one of the most liberating experiences of my life. Rad on his back, the pillows from my couch hastily shoved underneath his hips, his legs up on my shoulders. He braced himself against the brick hearth, and I fucked him in a way I hadn't fucked anybody in years. It was wild and frantic and fun. It seemed so perfect, somehow an inevitable and obvious conclusion to having him show up on my porch with a pickaxe in his hand.

As it turned out, sex with a crazy person was a hell of a lot of fun.

We found our way into the shower next, where we took turns washing each other.

Lather.

Rinse.

Repeat.

"You know," he said as he pushed me back against the cold tile wall, "we're just going to get dirty again."

"Then I guess we'll have to take another shower." Although given the size of my water heater, we'd probably be facing a cold shower the second time around.

He pushed his knees in between my thighs, causing me to spread my legs. "I think it's my turn."

"I can handle that."

He laughed. "You're lucky. You won't be hitting your head on that damn brick fireplace. If I were staying past tomorrow, we'd have to pad the damn thing."

"I don't think my dad was thinking of sex when he put it in."

"Obviously not." He turned to shut off the water. "Let's use the bed this time."

"Right." But I wasn't actually thinking about the bed. I was thinking about the hearth. The brick hearth, which my father had put in.

"Josh, where are the clean towels?"

"There wasn't a hearth," I said.

"What?"

Why hadn't I thought of it sooner? "When Winston and Alton built this cabin! There wasn't a hearth. That wasn't added until later."

He stood there in the thick steam of the bathroom, water beading in the course hair on his chest, staring at me in surprise. "So you're saying—"

"It's buried under the hearth!"

I grabbed a towel on my way past him, hastily wiping the water out of my eyes and off my chest as I headed for the living room. I didn't bother with clothes. He had joked that we were just going to get dirty again, but he hadn't known at the time how right he was.

I figured it would be easier to dig over to the corner, burrowing underneath the hearth, than to break up the bricks. Still naked, I stepped down into the shallow hole Rad had made. The soil was cool against my bare feet. I crouched down and inspected the space between the dirt foundation and the remaining floorboards. There was about a two-inch gap between them. I tried to slide my hand between them, to feel for the buried money, but the space was too small for me to reach in very far.

"I need something to dig with."

There wasn't enough room to use the shovel at the angle I would need. He handed me the crowbar instead. I couldn't swing it in the space I had, but I used it to dig the dirt out of the way, burrowing toward the northeast corner of the room.

Finally, the gap was big enough for me to slide my hand in. It took only a minute of feeling around before I found it.

It was an old-fashioned cigar box. I handed it to Rad with a feeling of hushed reverence. I was suddenly distinctly aware of our lack of clothing. It seemed somehow disrespectful.

Rad was silent as he opened the box. On the very top was an envelope. The name "Alton" was written across it. It was still sealed.

I noticed how Rad's hand shook as he held it.

"Looks like Winston wanted to say goodbye," I said.

Rad nodded. He put the unopened letter aside. Underneath was a strange collection of items: a folded, monogrammed handkerchief, a feather, a single cuff link. Items that had once meant something to two young lovers. Items that were now nothing more than lost memories. The pocketwatch was there as well. There were other letters, not in envelopes, love notes they'd exchanged throughout their relationship.

We didn't read them.

There was a picture, brittle with age, but still clear: two young men, standing against a nondescript wall. Not smiling. Not touching. I imagined I could see the strain of hiding their love in their tense postures and their sad eyes.

Underneath it all was the cash, but it hardly mattered. I could see now what Rad had meant when he'd said it wasn't about the money. The box held memories. It held what remained of a doomed and forbidden life.

It brought a lump to my throat.

"Thank you," Rad said, his voice not much more than whisper. When he looked up at me, I could see in his eyes the same sadness I felt. "This will mean a lot to him."

"I'm glad I could help."

He carefully returned the items to their box. He closed it and set it aside. He glanced around at the torn-up floor. "If you want to send me the bill—"

"Don't worry about it," I said. "I can afford to fix it. Besides, it was worth it."

He smiled at me. "I'm glad you think so." He reached out and took my hand. "It felt kind of like an adventure, didn't it?"

I pulled him into my arms. "*You're* the adventure."

I had to rinse off again in the shower, but then I led him into the bedroom. It was different, the second time around. Somehow, the contents of the box had changed everything. We were quiet and slow. There was a tenderness between us that hadn't been there before. We made love, as if it was the last chance either of us would ever have. As if we could make up for everything that had happened to Alton and Winston. As if we could give back what they had lost.

We made love as if it could somehow change the world.

Maybe it could.

I woke early. The sky outside my bedroom window was just beginning to turn a pale shade of gray, and for the first time in months — maybe years — I was excited to greet the day.

I made coffee and sat down at my computer, and I started to write.

I'd taken a wrong turn in chapter three. It was suddenly so obvious, I wondered how I'd failed to see it before. I also thought maybe it was time to throw my adventure-seeking character a curveball. A bit of tweaking, some deleting, some re-writing. Yes, I had a long way to go, but as the sunlight began to fill my tiny cottage, I began to feel confident. It was like being reborn.

"Are you always up so early?" Rad asked from the hallway.

"Not always."

He was already dressed. He went into the kitchen and poured himself a cup of coffee. He came in and sat down across from me at the table.

It was strange — not as uncomfortable as some of the other mornings after I'd had in my life, but still a bit awkward. "I need to get going," he said at last. "My flight home leaves in a few hours."

"Is there any way you can stay?"

He shook his head. "Not without losing my job. Plus, my dog's in the kennel. They're expecting me back."

"I see." Of course he couldn't drop everything just to hang out with me having sex. Still, I was sorry to see him go. Just being with him made me feel young.

He smiled at me, and I had an uncomfortable feeling he could read my mind. He pulled his chair over next to mine. "Josh," he said, leaning close to look into my eyes, "are you still interested in a change of scenery?"

"Maybe. Why?"

"Well, I was thinking, you can write anywhere, can't you? I know your home is in San Diego, but you can go anywhere. Just bring your laptop along, right?"

"Where are you suggesting?"

He smiled nervously. "How do you feel about Moab?"

I couldn't help but smile back at him. The thought made my heart beat a bit faster. It made my stomach fill with butterflies once again. Still, I barely knew him. "Are you asking me to move in with you?"

"No!" he said vehemently. Then he laughed. "No," he said again, gentler this time. "I'm asking if you'd like to come visit. My apartment's small, but I think we could manage."

"When?"

"As soon as you can."

"For how long?"

He smiled. He leaned closer and put one of his arms around my neck. His lips brushed mine. "For as long as it feels like an adventure."

I didn't know how long that would be, but I was more than ready to find out.

Apartment 14 and the Devil Next Door

Dedication

Many thanks to Sue, who gave me the idea.

Chapter One

As our plane prepared to land in Moab, Utah, I began to wonder if I'd lost my mind. Only three days ago, I'd been holed up in my Oregon cabin, lonely and frustrated and depressed, trying to make some progress on my latest novel. And now? I was following a man I barely knew to a city I'd never seen in order to live with him for an indefinite period of time.

Indefinite.

At that moment, the word seemed to describe every single aspect of my life, from the ending of the book I still needed to finish to my exact relationship with Radcliffe Fox, the man who'd so thoroughly screwed up my life in the best possible way. We'd only known each other three days. We'd been lovers for less than twenty-four hours. And yet here I was, throwing caution to the wind, following him on the grandest adventure I'd had in years.

Next to me, Rad ducked his head to peer out the window of the small commuter plane we'd boarded in Salt Lake City. He'd been restless and impatient as a kid the entire length of the flight from Portland to Salt Lake, but now that his hometown was in sight, he was calm. My anxiety, on the other hand, had grown with each passing mile until I thought I'd choke on it.

Rad turned to smile at me in a way that made me flush. "Almost there."

"Good."

He nudged my knee with his. "Stop worrying."

"Who said anything about being worried?"

"I can tell."

He was right, of course, but I had no way to voice my misgivings. I didn't know him well enough to start gushing about my lifetime's worth of insecurities.

You don't know him well enough to talk to him, yet you're planning to live with him? Great idea.

It took only a few minutes to collect our bags in Moab's tiny airport, and then we emerged into the scorchingly dry heat of the high desert in August. After only a few breaths, I felt as if my lungs would dry up in my chest and blow away with my next exhalation. I imagined my body's moisture being leeched away by the almost imperceptible breeze blowing from the west, my skin cracking and peeling like old paint. I imagined teetering down the street with a cane.

Rad wore a broad grin as he led me across the parking lot. "Man, it's good to be home."

I glanced around. This didn't look like anybody's home. Only a couple of small, squat buildings hunched in the middle of miles of dirt and sagebrush. "Where's the town?"

"Eighteen miles south of here."

He led me to a Jeep Wrangler that looked as old and rickety as I felt. There was no telling what color it was supposed to be. Its paint had faded to the same pale brown as the desert, and its roof and doors were both MIA. Layers of duct tape covered cracks in the leather seats.

"We'll drop our bags at the apartment," Rad informed me, "then pick up Yashe. And after that, I'll take you downtown for dinner. You can meet the gang."

The gang.

That one word was enough to amplify my anxiety. I'd stupidly pictured our time together being untainted by any outside influences, but I realized now how foolish that assumption was. Rad was young and vibrant, restless and wild, a veritable free spirit in a city full of tourists and wanderers. Of course he had a whole pack of friends. I wondered briefly what they'd be like, and immediately the answer popped into my brain: young. They'd be young. And me, the graying elder—the ancient outsider, lurking around their periphery. Sure, I was only forty-two, but next to Rad, I felt ancient. While sitting on the plane, we'd browsed the music on each other's phones. I hadn't heard of most of the bands he listened to, and he'd laughingly referred to my music as "classics."

Once again, I wondered if I was making the biggest mistake of my life.

We tossed our bags into the back seat and climbed into the Jeep. The Utah sun was bright and hot on my Oregon-cooled skin. The red-brown desert stretched out around us, barren, yet gloriously bold and beautiful beneath the perfect, cloudless blue sky. I buckled myself into the passenger seat, and Rad turned the key in the ignition. The engine was so loud, I practically had to shout to be heard over it.

"How old are you, anyway?"

He grinned knowingly at me, somehow managing to make fun of me and my question without saying a word. In the sunlight, his eyes were the same silver-green as the dusky sagebrush growing in tight clumps around the edge of the parking lot. "Twenty-six."

Sixteen years my junior. A couple of years older than the man Roger had left me for, but not by much. Part of me wanted to yell to the world that this man found me attractive. To rent billboards and set up a Facebook account, just so I could brag about my new lover.

The other half of me was still sure I should have stayed sequestered in my cabin back in Oregon.

"Stop worrying," Rad said again as he ground the Jeep into gear.

I didn't bother to deny it this time.

The hills became more pronounced and the vegetation more frequent as we rattled down the road. Twenty-five wind-blown minutes after leaving the airport, we arrived in Moab. Evidence of the region's bustling tourist industry lay on all sides. Jeeps, ATVs, and mountain bikes for rent. River rafting. Horse riding. Hotels, motels, campgrounds, and RV parks. Outdoor outfitters and companies promising every kind of adventure imaginable in Arches and Canyonlands National Parks and the surrounding regions. Scattered among them were the usual staples: grocery stores, fast food chains, independent diners and bars, and plenty of coffee shops.

"Have you ever been to Arches?" Rad asked.

"Nope. I've been skiing in Park City, but that's the extent of my travels in Utah."

He laughed. "Oh man, that might as well be in another state. It's a whole different world down here."

He turned off the main road and a minute later and parked in front of a small apartment complex. He led me to the door of apartment number fourteen. "Everybody here's pretty friendly. We have a pool around back, and— why the hell is my door unlocked?"

The answer to that question became evident the minute we walked inside. A man waited inside. He was tall and built, with neat black hair and perfectly arched eyebrows. Older than Rad, but younger than me. He looked like some kind of god.

No.

He looked too devious to be called a god. His eyes practically glowed with ill-intent. This man was definitely the devil in human skin.

"Hey, babe!" he said, taking Rad's hand and pulling him close. "Glad you're home." He wrapped long, muscular arms around Rad and squeezed his ass while nuzzling his neck. "I thought I'd give you a proper welcome."

Rad laughed, leaning into the embrace, tilting his head to allow better access to his neck. "Have you been waiting long?"

"Just long enough to think of all the possible ways we could celebrate your return." He stopped short as his eyes fell on me. I was pretty sure I saw the flames of hell burning in his pupils. "Who's this?"

Rad turned to face me, his cheeks red, but his eyes still full of laughter. "This is Joshua Franklin Hill."

"The writer?"

"Yeah."

The man's eyes widened in surprise. "You brought him home with you?"

"Yeah. Josh, this is Wren."

"Uh…" Proper manners dictated that I say something polite, like "pleased to meet you," but I couldn't follow through. I wasn't pleased to meet the devil. Not one bit.

Wren released Rad and came toward me, smiling in a way that made my ears burn. I hurriedly switched my duffel to my left hand in order to hold out my right, thinking he wanted to shake but he moved past it, stepping into my personal space to kiss me on the cheek. He snaked one arm around my waist, and I nearly jumped out of my skin as he grabbed my ass, much as he'd done to Rad.

"Fantastic," he breathed, moving his lips from my cheek to my ear. "I had no idea you were bringing somebody home for us to play with."

Us?

"Wait a minute," I said, putting a hand on his chest to push him away. I felt like a fool. I hadn't specifically asked Rad if he was single, but I'd assumed, after being invited to stay with him, that he didn't already have another man occupying his bed.

Of course, Wren wasn't a man. He was clearly a sign of the apocalypse.

"What's going on?" I asked Rad.

He shook his head dismissively. "Ignore him," he said.

"Ignore me?" Wren said, all mock indignation. "But, babe—"

"Cool it," Rad said, pushing between Wren and me with obvious exasperation. "You're going to scare him off before we even have dinner."

Wren laughed, but didn't appear dissuaded. "So, after dinner, then?" he asked, trying to pull Rad closer to him again. I was glad to see that this time, Rad resisted. "Is he a top or a bottom?"

"Either," Rad said.

"Excellent."

I gulped, wondering how I'd gotten myself into this. I'd been involved in a three-way once before, but that had been in college and had involved the liberal use of alcohol and poppers. It wasn't an experience I was anxious to repeat—especially not with Satan's identical twin. And it was painfully clear that Wren, with his mischievous eyes and solid build, knew my newfound lover better than I did. I winced at the thought of having to disrobe and stand naked next to his muscular body. Nothing good could come of that. I'd certainly suffer by comparison, and I didn't want to risk falling out of the circle, being left on the outside, watching as they shared an intimacy I'd never be part of.

I resisted the urge to hang my head. It seemed every assumption I'd made about what Rad wanted to happen between us was wrong. I wanted to turn and walk out. To fly back to Oregon.

But then Rad stepped closer to me. He took my hand. "Wren, listen," he said with the tone of a teacher addressing a recalcitrant pupil, "Josh's generation isn't into that kind of thing."

I was glad for his attempt to thwart Wren, but not so glad for the reminder of my seniority. "I'm not that old, you know!"

Wren winked at me. "Not too old at all."

Rad shook his head. "Josh is really old-fashioned. He doesn't jump into bed with guys he doesn't know."

Wren raised his eyebrows, glancing between Rad and I, as if waiting for the punch line. "Right. Because you guys have so much history. You've know each other, what? Three days now?"

"That's different," Rad told him, moving to wrap his arm possessively around my waist. "Josh and I had an adventure together, you know? An experience. Like," he smiled at me, "a magical moment."

Wren's eyebrows moved higher on his forehead. "A moment?"

"Yeah."

Wren laughed. "Well, maybe I'll have a 'moment' with him too."

"It doesn't work that way."

"It could."

"Wren?" Rad said, his low tone underlining his seriousness.

"Yeah."

"Listen to me: this isn't your moment."

"Maybe after dinner—"

"There won't be any moments tonight. Or tomorrow either."

"What about next week?"

"That'll be up to Josh. But for right now, you're excluded from all moments. Got it?"

Wren sighed, holding up his hands in amused exasperation. "All right, all right. I'll let you keep him to yourself for a while."

"Thank you. We'll see you downtown later, all right?"

"Is that your not-so-subtle way of telling me to get the hell out?"

"It is."

Wren shook his head. Whether he was annoyed or simply perplexed, I couldn't tell. "Man," he mumbled as he headed for the door. "Go away for three days and come back in a monogamous relationship. Who would have thought—" The rest of it was lost behind the slam of the door.

Rad turned to me with a mute apology in his eyes. "I didn't expect him to be here."

"I gathered that."

"He comes on a bit strong, I know, but he's not a bad guy."

Right. Evil incarnate, maybe, but not bad once you get to know him. "And you guys…"

He sighed. "Yeah. Occasionally."

"'Occasionally'?" I repeated, feeling as if the word were fraught with peril.

"We've known each other since college. Lived together for a while, but that was years ago. Now he lives in number thirteen—"

"Number thirteen?"

"Yes."

As if I needed more proof that he was the stuff of my nightmares. "So, he lives right next door?"

"Right."

"And you still sleep with him?"

"Like I said — occasionally."

I wondered if his definition of 'occasionally' was different from my own. Were we talking a few times a year? Once a month? A few times a week? "Great," I muttered.

Rad grinned, stepping closer. "You don't need to worry about him."

"Who said I was worried?"

His smile grew. He reached down and took my duffel, which I still held clutched in my left hand. He dropped it unceremoniously to the floor and pushed me back against the wall. "I can practically hear those gears turning in that big brain of yours. Spilling out all the possible scenarios, spinning away like a movie projector, filling your head with so many thoughts and images, you can't remember which ones make sense and which ones don't." He kissed my jaw and began unbuttoning my jeans. "How about if I give you something else to think about?"

My heart kicked into gear. A pleasing warmth surged in my groin as he pulled my pants open and slid them down my hips. "Uh…" But what about later? What about that god damn devil living next door, just waiting to get naked with Rad, or with me, or with both of us at once? What about "occasionally"? What about—?

"Stop thinking," Rad whispered into my ear as his fingers teased over my half-engorged cock. "Stop worrying. Stop assuming." He caressed me, coaxing my erection to life. "Can you do that for me? Can you turn off the projector?"

I swallowed and tried to nod, but his touch was already having the intended effect. I could barely think of anything at all except how good it felt. "Yes."

"Good." His continued ministrations felt like a reward. His lips warmed my ear, his whiskers tickling my cheek. "This can be whatever you want it to be, Josh. Whatever *we* want it to be. Just sit back and relax and let the adventure unfold."

It sounded so simple. So logical. So utterly liberating. "Okay."

And without another word, he sank to his knees. He sucked me in deep, and I let it all go. I forgot about Roger and his lover and my unfinished novel and my nagging agent and Wren and what exactly 'occasionally' might mean. I lost myself in the pure erotic joy of Rad's mouth moving on my cock. I threaded my fingers through his thick, unruly curls, and let him suck me until I thought my knees would give out from the pleasure. It was simple, yet strangely intense, and I found myself panting, moaning, thrusting hard into his waiting mouth, feeling as if every doubt and insecurity and fear could be channeled into my aching loins and poured down his willing throat. My orgasm, when it came, tore from my mouth with a ragged cry and left me shaking and breathless.

Rad rose to his feet, his lips swollen and red and slick. I pulled him close and kissed him deeply, tasting my semen on his tongue, feeling his arousal in the way he pressed against me, judging his sheer amusement by the curve of his lips.

"That was so fucking hot," he whispered when I broke the kiss.

"Yes, it was."

"Quick: tell me what you're thinking about right this second."

"About returning the favor."

He laughed. "Good." He sobered quickly, staring intently into my eyes, as if searching for the anxieties he'd seen there earlier. He must have liked what he found, because he smiled. "See?" he said, putting his hand against my cheek and brushing his thumb over my brow, as if soothing away the worry lines. "Isn't this way better?"

"It is. You're absolutely right."

"Of course I am. Now, are you ready for dinner?"

"If you are."

"Definitely. I'm starving. And when we get back here," he lowered his eyelashes flirtatiously, "I'll show you the bedroom."

"I can hardly wait."

And so once again, I followed him to his car which no longer seemed old and beaten. It seemed ideally suited to its owner and their locale. We drove into town as the sun began to dip below the horizon, throwing a shadowy blanket of red and orange over the heat of the desert, tinting the air with the promise of twilight's cooling touch. I felt loose-jointed and giddy, alive, yet sated, unable to stop smiling after the surprising strength of my orgasm. Next to me, Rad chatted amiably, throwing me flirtatious glances and waving to people he knew as he pointed out local landmarks, favorite diners, and places he'd worked, and it was absolutely perfect. Bumping down the road in his rickety Jeep, I felt young and completely at ease. Worry no longer found sustenance in my heart.

It's an adventure, I told myself. *He's an adventure. And he's exactly what you need.*

Chapter Two

We made one stop on the way to dinner, to pick Rad's dog up from the kennel. Yashe was a golden lab, although her snout was almost completely white from age. Her movements were slow, but she wagged her tail in wild delight upon seeing Rad. He lifted her into the back seat of his Jeep because she couldn't make the jump any more, and we headed toward the heart of Moab.

"Why not leave her with Wren, if he lives right next door?"

"She's never liked him much. She tends to growl every time she sees him."

More proof that Wren was actually evil incarnate. I suddenly wanted to hug Rad's dog. "What will you do with her while we eat?"

"They're dog friendly where we're going. She'll hang out on the patio with us."

"They let dogs into the restaurant?"

"Only the good ones, right Yashe?" He reached back to scratch the dog's ears before saying to me, "I go back to work tomorrow. I thought maybe you'd want to drive me there so you could have the Jeep."

I hadn't thought about how I'd get around town. In truth, I hadn't thought about much. On Monday morning, he'd pounded on my cabin door, waking me from what felt like half a lifetime of hibernation. On Tuesday, we'd torn a hole in my living room floor in search of his grandfather's long lost mementoes. Now it was Wednesday evening and I was watching the sun set over the Utah desert. We'd managed to nail the floorboards back in place before rushing off to the airport to secure me a spot on his flight home, but that was it. "What about the box?" I asked. "When will you give it to your grandfather?"

"I'll drive up to Provo on my next day off." He smiled to himself at the thought. "Wonder what he'll say when I tell him about you." He shifted nervously in his seat. For the first time since I'd met him, he seemed unsure. "I feel like I should invite you to go with me, but I think he'd rather not have an audience this time, you know?"

"That's fine. I understand."

"Next time, though, okay? He's the only member of my family I'm really close to. I really do want you to meet him. Just, not the day I take him the box."

I was flattered that he wanted to introduce me at all. "Whenever you're ready."

He smiled over at me, and I knew I'd said the right thing.

The restaurant he took me to was what my ex liked to call American unchic shabby — rough wooden tables and chairs, peanuts in bins by the front door, AC/DC playing on crackling speakers, and a menu full of burgers and everything fried. The one nice surprise was the beer. The restaurant was also a brewery, and Rad promptly ordered a collection of samples — which I learned was called a "flight" — so I could try everything. We joined a group of his friends in the corner by a dartboard and a foosball table. An open door led to a patio, where two other dogs lazily greeted us, along with Wren, who'd apparently arrived only moments before.

I did my best to smile, even though I felt sure there must be little red horns hidden under his immaculate hair.

Rad introduced me to everybody, although I knew it'd take me a while to keep their names straight. I was surprised to see that my initial presumption that they'd all be in their twenties was wrong. I guessed most of them to be in their thirties. Maybe none of them were quite as old as me, but I felt sure a couple of them came close. They all seemed friendly enough, too. I couldn't tell which fact stunned Rad's gang of buddies more: that Rad had brought me back to

Moab with him, or that he'd convinced me to let him dig up my floor.

"So you're the author he was going on about?" one of the men said.

"Yep."

"You write those Alex Daring books?"

"I do."

"And you actually let Rad pull up boards and dig a damn hole, right there in your living room?"

"I was reluctant at first, I admit. But he was persuasive."

"I won him over," Rad interjected. He held his hand out to the other man. "So pay up."

The man laughed and dug out his wallet, still shaking his head at me. "I was sure you'd say no."

"I knew Rad could convince him," Wren said, draping his arm over Rad's shoulder. "He could sell sand in the desert and convince you it was water."

"Sure, you said he could convince him," one of the women — I thought her name was Sasha — said. "But nobody thought he'd drag a famous author all the way back to Moab with him just to prove his point."

"That's not the only reason I brought him back with me," Rad said, winking at me as he disentangled himself from Wren.

We ate dinner and drank beer, and then discovered quite by accident that Rad and I made a lethal foosball team. We won several games before I tired of it and gave up my spot as Rad's partner to Wren. As much as I hated to let him angle into my place, I was older than them, and used to getting to bed by ten. After a day of traveling plus losing an hour flying one time zone to the east, I was ready to sit on my ass for a while and drink my beer. I pulled up a stool next to Sasha and ordered another drink.

"So," she said, leaning close, as if sharing a great secret. "You're the guy who might finally land Rad, huh?"

"Uh…" I glanced over at him, watched him laugh as he and Wren scored another goal. "I got the impression plenty of people had done that before me."

"Ha! Are you kidding? Plenty of us have tried, and we've all failed miserably. He's like the white whale. Cute as hell, but no monster ego to contend with. Athletic, but not snotty about it. He's funny and friendly, but not a schmooze. Plus, he manages to stay employed without giving in to the man or letting go of the whole 'free-spirit' vibe. He's basically the perfect catch, but nobody's landed him yet."

"Nobody?"

"Not really."

That didn't fit at all with what I thought about him. Then again, what I knew about him could have fit in one of the empty shot glasses sitting in the middle of the table. "I got the impression he was pretty casual about relationships."

"Sex, you mean?"

I nodded, proud of myself for managing to not blush.

She laughed. "Sure, he lets guys pick him up from time to time. But I've never seen him show any real interest before. It's more like he's doing them a favor. A couple of nights sharing their bed — never at his place — and then he's always on his own again."

"Wow. That surprises me."

"Yeah. And it's not like most of us haven't tried, guys and girls alike."

A cheer went up from the foosball table. Rad and Wren had scored again. Wren leaned close to whisper something in Rad's ear. Rad laughed, but waved at me as their opponent got ready to reset the ball. "What about Wren?" I asked. "I got the feeling they'd been together. You know. *Occasionally.*" Which in my mind, translated to way too many god damn times.

She laughed. "Jealous?"

I winced. "Is it that obvious?"

"You shouldn't be."

"That's what Rad said."

"He's right."

"But—"

"No, I get it. I mean, yeah, Wren can get Rad into bed. He succeeds more than any of the rest of us, believe me. Probably the only person in Moab who's seen Rad's bedroom. But I think that's only because they've known each other for years. It's more about being comfortable and easy than because Rad gives a shit. The next morning, he always sends Wren back home. Rad won't ever commit, and even worse, he never gets jealous of Wren's other lovers, no matter how hard Wren tries." She shook her head. "No. Wren's worked harder than anyone to land Moab's most eligible bachelor, but so far, no luck. And now Rad runs off for a weekend and comes home with you? Wren must be losing his mind over it."

She may have been trying to reassure me, but mostly, she was making me worry. "Maybe he'll send me away after a couple of nights too," I said, hoping it wasn't true.

She shook her head. "I don't think so. I've never seen him act like this before."

"Like what?"

"Well, letting you stay at his place, for one thing. That's not like him. And then bringing you here to show you off to his friends. And the way he keeps watching you." And sure enough, when I looked over, I caught Rad glancing my way again. "He's driving Wren crazy, and he doesn't even care." She nudged me with her elbow. "What'd you do? Cast a spell on him? Drop a love potion in his drink?"

"No, I...." I let him dig up my living room floor. He told me he liked my gray hair. We unearthed lost treasure. "We had a moment."

"That must have been one hell of a moment," she said. "Wouldn't mind having one of those with somebody myself."

The foosball game ended and Rad begged out of another one, choosing instead to come and hang his arm over my shoulder. "Ready to go home?" he asked quietly.

I liked that he called it 'home', as if it belonged to both of us, even though I hadn't yet spent a single night at his place. "Definitely."

My exhaustion caught up with me somewhere between the restaurant and apartment fourteen. I was dead on my feet by the time he led me into his bedroom.

"I think I'm too old for late nights and that much beer after traveling all day," I told him.

He turned a sexy smile my way and pulled me into a kiss. "Are you too old for this?" he teased, pressing his hard, lithe body against mine.

My weariness faded in a hurry. "Not yet, I'm not."

"Prove it."

I like to think I succeeded. I may have fallen into a dead sleep two minutes after it was over, but in my defense, I wasn't the only one.

Chapter Three

I chose to sleep in the next day, and let Rad drive himself to work. I rose shortly before noon and fired up my laptop. There wasn't room in Rad's apartment for an office, per se, but I made a spot to work in his tiny living room, not far from the window-unit air conditioner, with a view of the pool, and beyond that, the rocky sandstone hills rolling into the distant desert. Yashe rested happily at my feet. By the time Rad returned from work and dragged me into the bedroom for some pre-dinner festivities, I'd finished two more chapters.

Our first week together passed in a strange pattern of idle days and frantically sweaty nights. It'd been more years than I cared to count since I'd experienced such sheer joy at the mere sight of somebody. We barely knew each other, and yet there was no denying the quickening between us as the days passed. The giddiness of knowing neither of us could wait to get our hands on the other. The shared sense of mystery and confusion as we learned our way around each other's bodies, not only in bed, but in the confined space of his apartment. Learning to negotiate shower time in the mornings, and space in the kitchen during meal time, took patience, and yet we found an easy rhythm together. Some evenings we spent at the pub with his friends. Some we spent swimming in the small pool behind our apartment. Others we spent curled up on the couch together, finding all the ways our sixteen year age difference mattered, and all the ways it didn't. He laughed at me constantly, claiming that everything I did, from making him dinner to choosing plain coffee over lattes was old-fashioned, but I learned to take it in stride.

Nearly two weeks later, on his first day off after my arrival, Rad took the box we'd found under my living room floor and drove north to Provo to visit his grandfather, leaving me stranded in apartment fourteen.

Sharing an apartment hadn't been a problem yet, but sharing a car had already grown wearisome. Most days, I drove him to work and had the Jeep for any errands I wanted to run, but now, with him gone for the day, I decided something had to give.

The obvious solution was to buy a car. I didn't need anything fancy. Something used would do. I had plenty of money. My one concern was that buying a vehicle would be a not-so-subtle indication that I planned to stay for more than a few more days. For myself, I was more than ready to make that commitment, but was Rad? I was afraid to ask. So far, I felt our sudden cohabitation was going better than I could ever have hoped, but that didn't mean he felt the same way.

I spent the afternoon wondering how to bring it up. By the time he returned from Provo late that afternoon, I'd imagined a hundred different scenarios, each one more hurtful than the last, from Rad being shocked and appalled by my desire to stay to him laughing in my face and telling me to leave. I was glad when he got home, partly because it gave me something else to think about.

"How'd it go?" I asked.

"I don't know." He didn't meet my gaze. Instead, he tossed his keys onto the table by the door and pushed past me, into the kitchen.

Our greetings were usually warm and affectionate. His sudden distance surprised me. It felt like an ominous foreboding, after my day of imagined break-ups. "What happened? Did something go wrong?" I asked, following him.

"It's hard to say." He turned his back on me and opened the refrigerator. "It was either wonderful, or it was awful. Maybe he'll have his closure now, or maybe seeing what was in the box only made things worse. I can't decide if giving it to him was the right thing to do or not. He was happy at first, but then…" He stared into the fridge, searching for I knew not what. "He read Winston's letter, and he lost it. He completely fell apart. It was terrible. I've never seen my grandfather cry like that. He…."

His voice faltered a second time. I was confused, until I noticed the tension in his neck and shoulders, and the whiteness of his knuckles on the refrigerator handle. I finally realized why he was staring so determinedly into the fridge: not because he wanted anything out of it, but because he didn't want me to see how upset he was.

I reached past him and gently closed the appliance door. I put my hand on his shoulder. "I'm sorry."

He hesitated only a moment before turning and allowing me to pull him into my arms. He clung to me, trembling as he fought to keep his feelings at bay. "You should have seen him, Josh. It was heartbreaking. I had no idea what to do. At first I was mad at Winston. I felt like whatever he said in that letter, it must have been mean or hateful. But now…" He took a deep, quavering breath. "I don't know. I don't know how to feel. If my grandfather had stayed with Winston, I wouldn't be here. I literally wouldn't exist. But he was left with so much regret."

"He had a tough choice to make. Harder than either of us can imagine, I think."

"But did he make the right one?"

"I don't think it was a matter of right or wrong. It was far more complex than that."

"But why? Why did it have to be that way at all?"

"It was a different time." It was a weak explanation, I knew, but the only one I had. I held him, stroking his hair, kissing the side of his head, and slowly, he regained his composure. Eventually, he sighed. He put his arms around me and settled more comfortably against me.

"It seems so unfair."

"It does," I agreed.

"It doesn't have to be that way for us, right?"

"No. Like you said that first day, this can be whatever we want it to be."

He nodded, his unruly curls brushing my cheek as he did. "Thank you."

"For what?"

"I don't know. Everything." He kissed my quickly and let me go. He opened the fridge again, but this time he took out a can of root beer. "How was your day? Better than mine, I assume."

"It was fine. I didn't do much." Just spent the day imagining all the ways you might break up with me.

"Did you go anywhere?"

"Well—"

He smacked the heel of his hand against his temple. "I'm being an idiot. You would have had to walk. I'm sorry. You know, I have a bike. It's in storage, and I'm sure the tires are flat, but it'd be better than nothing."

Exactly the opening I needed, if I had the courage to take it. I swallowed hard, steeling my nerve. "Well, I know this may seem sudden, but I was thinking about buying a car. If, well you know…" I watched him, waiting for him to look shocked or appalled or horrified. "If you don't mind me staying a bit longer."

To my relief, none of those heartbreaking expressions appeared on his face. His lips spread into a broad, open smile. He set his can of soda aside and stepped close again to wrap his arms around my neck. His kiss was slow and deep and full of promise, and all my doubts disappeared.

"I think that's a great idea."

Chapter Four

The very next day, I bought a used Subaru Outback. I also began jogging early in the morning, before the day had a chance to heat up. For the first time in years, writing didn't feel like a chore, and I made excellent progress on my book. I worked when Rad worked, and on his days off, he showed me the sights. We went on hikes in Arches and Canyonlands National Parks, and in the La Sal Mountains. We camped deep in the desert. Rad took me on Jeep tours, and on a rafting trip down the Colorado River. I dropped ten pounds without even realizing it and had to buy new shorts. I wasn't used to the dry air yet, but I soaked up the heat, often basking in the sun like one of the desert's tiny, lightning-quick lizards. I knew the warnings about being aged by the sun, but I found it hard to believe. I'd never felt so young.

"You already look like one of us," Sasha said to me sometime in late September as we lounged around the patio at the brewpub.

I didn't have to ask what she meant. Outdoor enthusiasts flocked to Moab by the thousands, and some — like Rad and his entire group of friends — never left. It wasn't that they were dirty, but they all tended toward a certain bronzed scruffiness born of too much time in the sun and the wind. They were hard-baked, stubbly, dusty in the creases, prone to dreadlocks and tie-dyes, and seemed to wear either Tevas or hiking boots, regardless of the season. I'd only been in Moab for five weeks, and I was irrationally proud to join their ranks.

The one point of ongoing conflict between Rad and me was Wren. The man truly was the devil. He was drop-dead gorgeous, with a body to die for, and he knew it. Women and men both mooned after him, and he rejected very few of them. He spent the first few weeks after my arrival in Moab trying to make Rad jealous by parading a slew of lovers in front of us. When that didn't work, he altered his tactics.

And it quickly became clear that his new plan was to seduce me.

I didn't bother feeling flattered by his attentions. I wasn't his real target. I was only a means to an end. I had no doubt he would have tried to seduce Rad instead, given the chance, but there was rarely a time when Rad was home without me. I, however, was home without him for several hours at a time while he worked. Wren began stopping by the apartment in various states of undress, and he wasn't a bit shy about personal contact. Blocking his many advances was exhausting. I learned to avoid him by taking Yashe and my laptop elsewhere to work, but the man was persistent. He began timing his visits for shortly before Rad arrived home, and no matter how much I protested, no matter how hard I worked to stay out of his reach, I always felt guilty when Rad walked in the door. I always saw that question in his eyes, wondering if I'd finally allowed myself to be seduced.

"Come on," Wren pleaded one night in late October after we returned from the brewpub. He'd followed us inside, ostensibly to have one more beer with us, but when I came out of the restroom two minutes later, I found him on the couch next to Rad, stroking his thigh and whispering in his ear.

"What's going on?" I asked, even though I already knew. I tried to meet Rad's eyes, to see there what exactly he wanted to happen here, but he wouldn't meet my gaze.

It was Wren who answered me. "We were talking about all the ways we could work together to give you the night of your life." He reached out and took my hand, pulling me toward where they both sat on the couch. "Josh, you know the three of us could be great together, right?

"I told you," Rad said, still refusing to look at me. "Josh isn't into casual sex."

Wren sighed in exasperation. "What the hell does that even mean? What makes it 'casual' versus 'intimate'? We all know each other, right? We're all friends here." He put his arm around Rad again, leaning close to nuzzle his neck, and although Rad seemed more annoyed than turned on, he didn't push Wren away. "Come on, baby. It's been ages since we've been together. If you want it to be for Josh, it can be. Just stop pushing me away."

Finally, Rad glanced up at me, but I could read nothing in his pale green eyes. It was as if he'd locked me out, and I didn't know if it was because I hadn't said yes, or because I hadn't said no.

"This isn't a good night," I said, watching Rad carefully for some kind of sign. "Rad has to be up early, and I have a deadline to meet."

It was a lame excuse. We all knew it, but after only a bit of whining, Wren gave up and went home, leaving Rad and I in awkward silence.

I hated it. Our time together was otherwise perfect. Then Wren showed up and made things tense. Now especially, more than two months since we'd first met, as I felt the subtle shift between Rad and me — that indefinable deepening that told me this wasn't a fling, that we could truly make this thing work between us — to have Wren step in with his seductive bullshit was almost more than I could bear. I pondered it as I brushed my teeth, then yielded the sink to Rad. I wanted the man out of our lives.

But did Rad want the same thing?

It was time for me to find out.

I sat on the edge of the bed and waited until he emerged from the bathroom.

"Let's talk."

He sighed. Not in annoyance, but the sad surrender of somebody facing the firing squad. He sat down next to me on the bed and put his head in his hands, tangling his fingers into his unruly hair. "I suppose we've put it off longer than we should have."

I nodded. Yes, we had. And yet even now, having done the only thing I knew how to do to start the conversation, I had no idea where to truly begin. For better or worse, he spoke before I could formulate words.

"The thing is," he said, his voice strangely muffled by his posture, "we never said we were going to be exclusive, right?"

"No. Not really."

"And if we think about it logically, it's all bullshit. The entire idea that we can own another person, or make rules for them to suit our own needs. Or that sex has to lead to intimacy, or that sex with somebody else has to mean the end of intimacy. Or that two people form a unit that's somehow special and sanctified. Those are old-fashioned ideas based on Judeo-Christian mores. They have nothing to do with human nature or human desire or the human condition. Right?"

My heart ached, but I forced myself to say, "Right."

"So, there you go. That's your answer."

I chewed on it for a minute, but finally shook my head. "That isn't an answer at all."

"Are you going to make me say it?"

"Yes." Even though I had a feeling hearing it would break my heart.

"Fine." He sighed again and dropped his hands. He finally faced me — really, truly faced me for the first time all evening — not with the guarded expression he'd worn when Wren was with us, but with his eyes so full of pain and anguish that I was taken aback. "I can't tell you what to do," he said, his voice hoarse.

I stared at him, trying to make the words he'd said match the expression in his eyes. Trying to make sense of the entire thing. I'd been sure he was trying to tell me that he wanted Wren — that he didn't want to be tied to me exclusively — and yet now, I wondered.

"Are you saying you want to bring Wren into bed with us, or not?"

"I'm saying what I've always said: it's up to you."

"It's up to *us*."

"Right. Well, it seems to me, if you agree that... that..." He rubbed his hands briskly over his thighs and turned away, as if searching the room for some other option. Finding nothing, he leaned forward again and clenched his hands between his legs. "If you agree that monogamy is a culturally-compelled patriarchal myth, and that it's contrary to human nature, then—"

"Rad, stop," I said, trying not to laugh. For the first time, I saw his philosophy degree at work. "I'm not asking for an in-depth discussion on the pros and cons of monogamy. If I want that, I'll buy a book."

He slumped. "Then I don't know what to say."

I took his hand and pulled him toward me. I made him meet my eyes. "It's easy. Stop talking in circles, and tell me what you want."

"What if what I want isn't fair?"

"To hell with fair." I put my hand against his whiskery cheek and leaned closer. I wanted to kiss him. To hold him. To offer the comfort he seemed to need, and yet I knew we had to deal with this first. "Do you want to sleep with Wren?"

His answer was immediate, and unwavering. "No." He shook his head. "No, I don't care about that. But..." He faltered, "if you want to—"

"I don't."

He stopped, his brow wrinkled in confusion. "You don't?"

"No."

Confusion gave way to disbelief. "Really?"

"Really."

"But, it's Wren. Everybody wants him. He's, you know... " He waved his hand futilely in the direction of apartment thirteen, as if trying to use a single gesture to sum up the undeniable charisma of evil's true form.

"I know what he is, but I'm not interested. The only reason we're talking about this at all is because I thought it was what you wanted."

"No!" He laughed with obvious relief, his shoulders finally relaxing as he let his anxieties go. "Oh my god, I can't believe it. I was so worried. I don't want to limit you. I don't want to be that person. I asked you here. I wanted you to feel like this was an adventure—"

"It is," I assured him. "I do."

"But now I'm telling you to stop. How is that fair? How is that right?"

"This isn't about right or wrong. It's about what you and I want, right here, right now. That's all. Maybe being exclusive is old-fashioned—"

"It is."

"But it's our choice to make."

He pondered that for a moment. Finally, he smiled and leaned closer, letting his lips play over mine. "You're right. And the simple truth is, I don't want to share you. Not right now. Especially not with him."

"That's all I needed to hear." I wrapped my arms around him and kissed him, reveling at the way he responded to my touch. His readiness as I lay him back on the bed, caressing him and undressing him. At the way he moaned as I lowered myself onto him, taking him in, moving on him, staring deep into his eyes as we made love.

"I never wanted him anyway. You, Radcliffe Fox, are all the adventure I need."

Chapter Five

October gave way to November. Pumpkins fled the grocery stores, making way for frozen turkeys and over-eager Christmas wreaths as the weather turned cold. I finished the latest venture of Alex Daring and promptly started another. Summers in the high desert were scorching, but it soon became clear that winter was going to be downright frigid. Rad and I still spent his days off hiking more often than not, but we began spending more nights home alone, cuddled together in the warmth of apartment fourteen. I was taken aback when he came home one afternoon and announced that his hours leading Jeep tours had been cut in half.

"I'm used to it," he told me with a resigned smile. "Fewer tourists, fewer tours. That's how it goes. It'll pick up again in the spring."

"But, what will you do?"

"I've been saving all summer. With any luck, I can make it through without having to resort to waiting tables."

I hesitated, stirring the pasta sauce simmering on the stove to buy myself time to think. We'd never talked about money before. We still paid for everything separately except for groceries, which we split in half. I'd offered to pay half the rent more than once, but he always declined, saying it was his apartment and I was his guest. But I didn't feel like a guest. Not anymore, at least. And in truth, I'd begun to dream of sharing a space that belonged to both of us—a space with more room, and maybe a yard for Yashe. More importantly, a place that wasn't right next door to Wren.

"I have plenty of money," I began tentatively.

"Josh, it's my name on the lease—"

"No, listen. What if we moved?"

"Are you talking about leaving Moab?"

I debated. "Not necessarily, no, although I still have the cabin in Oregon."

His expression was skeptical. "You want to spend the winter in *Oregon*? Your cabin's smaller than my apartment."

"True. And there's no heat."

"Yeah," he said with dry sarcasm. "Great idea. I don't know why I'm not packing already."

"It doesn't have to be Oregon."

"What does that mean?"

"I still have a condo in San Diego."

He shook his head. "No. Absolutely not. I could never live there."

"Okay," I conceded without surprise. I couldn't picture him being happy in a city that big. "Well, maybe it's time to talk about other options."

He leaned a hip against the counter and looked down at his well-worn hiking boots. "Are you trying to tell me you're tired of being here?"

"No!" But now that he said it, I started to worry. "Are you tired of me being here?"

"No…"

But he didn't sound as sure as I might have liked. I turned away again, ostensibly to stir the sauce, suddenly doubting myself. I swallowed. Cleared my throat. Finally took a deep breath and dove in. "What if we bought a house?"

I hoped it would be like when I'd suggested the car — that I'd have his sudden and enthusiastic support — but it quickly became clear it wasn't to be. Not this time. The silence was frightening. One second. Then another. And another. Finally, his voice dark and low: "Have you lost your mind?"

"I just thought—"

"I tell you that my hours have been cut in half — that I'll be stretched to make ends meet until spring — and you want to buy a fucking house?"

"I have money. And I've been thinking about selling the condo in San Diego anyway." It was the house I'd shared with Roger. If Rad had wanted to live there with me, I might have made it work, but without him, I had no reason to go back.

But Rad wasn't convinced. He crossed his arms over his chest. "I didn't invite you here to be my sugar daddy."

"Good, because I'm not that old."

"Damn it, Josh. I'm serious."

"So am I."

His jaw clenched. "No."

"Why not?"

"Why not? Because it's insane. I don't want to be tied down like that. Not at my age."

That hurt, no denying it. "So, your objection isn't to sharing a house. It's to sharing a house with me?"

"That's not what I said!"

"Fine," I said, turning away. "Forget I mentioned it."

I stood there, feeling as if he'd punched me in the gut, glowering at the unoffending pot of pasta sauce. Rad hadn't moved from his spot a few feet away, but I felt his angry stare between my shoulder blades. It was the closest we'd come to an argument in our three months together, and I was surprised at how much it upset me. We ate dinner in silence. He did the dishes while I flipped moodily through the channels on TV. Eventually, we climbed into bed, one of us on each side, neither of us reaching for the other.

I wanted to cry, which both surprised and scared me. In the weeks since we'd agreed to lock Wren out of our bedroom, things had changed between us. Or, at least, they'd changed for me. The thrill of new-found infatuation and lust had given way to something deeper. I mourned each morning when he left. I celebrated each afternoon when he returned. I looked forward every night to this time when we lay in bed together, whether we made love or not. And when we did...

Just the thought of it thrilled me. The sex between us had become unbelievable, often leaving me shaken to my core, awed and amazed at the way we seemed to merge into one glorious, beautiful being. This, more than anything, made me think he must feel the same way I did. What else but love could explain the ever-deepening intensity between us? What else could account for the way we both lost ourselves when we touched?

And yet now, I doubted everything.

"Josh?" he said softly.

"Yes."

He slid his hand across the bed, his skin hissing against the cotton sheets until I felt his fingers, warm yet hesitant on my arm. "Please tell me we're okay."

Were we? Part of me felt we were something way more than okay. We were spectacular. We were divine. We were in the process of falling hopelessly, madly, passionately in love. But then I remembered what he'd said earlier. *I don't want to be tied down.*

"I don't want to be your *guest*," I said, my voice tight.

"I know. But my credit isn't so good, and my income isn't steady. And my lease isn't up for six more months. And I don't want you to support me, Josh. Jesus, I can't allow that. And I know you mean well, but…" He swallowed. "It may sound silly, but Moab is my heart. The thought of leaving is like selling my soul."

Yes, I understood that. I'd never wanted to leave Moab anyway. I just wanted a space that belonged to us both. And I'd wanted to put distance between us and Wren, but it seemed I'd jumped the gun.

I took his hand and drew him across the bed into my arms. "Fine. But starting right now, I'm paying half the rent."

He nodded, his hair brushing my chin as he did. "That's fair."

It seemed like we should say more, but I was afraid. I felt as if we'd barely regained our footing on the sharp edge of an abyss. As if we'd somehow managed to avoid toppling in, but my heart still thundered from the nearness of the fall. I held him, trying to find the right words to say, until he shifted against me, sliding his leg between my thighs, moving his hand to my groin, his lips to my jaw.

"Josh," he whispered, suddenly breathless and impatient. "Please."

And then we were moving, kissing, caressing. Eventually shifting so we could both use our mouths on the other, moaning in unison, locked fervently together in our passion. And when it was over, we lay there, his head on my thigh, my head on his, trembling in each other's arms, yet miles apart.

I loved him. I worshipped him. I cherished him. I felt about him the way he felt about Moab, but I feared he'd never feel the same way about me. How could he? He was so young. I'd lived a life already. Loved a man and lost him. Moved on. Found Rad. I didn't want to waste another minute. I wanted to spend every single day I had left with him. But I was a fool, and not for the first time, I reeled at the thought of the sixteen years that separated us. At the realization that when I'd been graduating from high school, he'd still been in diapers. Why in the world would he want to tie himself to an old man like me?

Was any of this real? Or was he only passing time? And either way, did he know how much I loved him? Did he know how close he'd come to breaking my heart? I wanted to ask, but I suspected he wouldn't give me a sincere answer.

Or maybe I was afraid he would.

Chapter Six

December was a maddening mixture of heart-wrenching love and blinding insecurity. When we'd first met, I'd thought he was crazy. Now I feared I was the one losing my mind. I walked around in a daze, sometimes catching myself simply staring at Rad like a fool, other times fearing I'd lose all touch with reality and simply blurt out "I love you!" as we debated the pros and cons of sugared breakfast cereal in aisle four of the grocery store.

Shortly before Christmas, my madness reached an all new level as I left the bank. A light layer of snow frosted the ground. Glittering ornaments hung from streetlights. The stores and restaurants were all playing Christmas music. Rad and I had spent the previous evening watching *Miracle on 34th Street*. I'd never cared for it, but Rad had insisted, calling it a classic, like me, and my heart had swelled so big, I thought it would burst. And now, twelve hours later, I found myself staring stupidly into the window of the local jewelry store.

I could marry him.

The thought felt like a revelation. Like a gift. Like the most perfect idea I'd ever had. Even here in Utah, I could now legally make him my husband. I went inside and picked out a ring. I walked out of the store with the little felt box in my hand and a smile on my face.

Yes. I'd do this. I'd take him to one of our favorite spots in Arches on Christmas Day. I'd wait until sunset. And then I'd get down on my knee like some romantic sap in a movie. I'd declare my love for him out loud for the very first time, and I'd ask for his hand in marriage.

It was the perfect plan.

Except of course, it was me — old-fashioned and neurotic and stupidly in love with the most impossible man on the planet.

Of course, something had to go wrong.

The first blow to my fatal downfall came the next day. Rad was at work. I was parked in front of my laptop, my toes being comfortably warmed by Yashe's rear end as she napped — she could snore like a freight train — when my phone rang. I glanced at the screen to see who was calling, and had to do a double take.

Roger Buchanan.

Roger and I hadn't spoken since the previous spring when he'd left me for his twenty-four year old aerobics instructor. Why would he be calling me now?

"Hello?"

"Josh. Hey. It's me."

"I know."

He was silent, maybe searching for words. Maybe wondering if he should cut his losses and simply hang up. "I wanted to see you," he said at last. "I've been going by the house, but it seems like you're never home."

"No. I haven't been back there since..." Since he'd moved out. It felt like a lifetime ago. Our relationship had been over long before he'd dumped me. Long before he'd moved in with his younger lover. Ages and ages before Rad had pounded on my cabin door and asked if he could tear a hole in my living room floor. "I've been thinking about selling it, actually."

"I see."

We sat in awkward silence for a moment. I didn't hate him, but I didn't love him anymore either. I tried to keep my voice gentle as I said, "What do you need, Roger?"

"I don't even know, to be honest. I just wanted to hear your voice. I wanted to know how you are. If you're doing okay."

"I am. I'm good."

"Oh. Have you, um..."

"Yes. I've moved on."

"You met somebody?"

"I did."

"I see."

I waited, trying to decide what I was feeling. Wondering what he was feeling. I didn't miss him. I found it hard to believe he missed me. And yet, I heard something in his voice. An echo of regret that told me he was wondering what might have been.

"Brent left me."

It felt so sudden. So odd that he would call and reveal this to me, of all people. "Oh."

"I don't know, Josh. I was such a fool. I guess that's what I wanted to say. I'm not begging you to take me back or anything like that. But, I wanted you to know that I'm sorry. I was an idiot. I know things hadn't been great between us in a long time, but in hindsight…God, I don't even know how things got so fucked up, you know? I don't know how we ever got from point A to point D."

"Neither of us handled things as well as we might have."

"I guess we didn't. But, you're really doing all right?"

"I'm great."

"You're happy?"

"I am."

"I'm glad." He laughed without much humor. "Just don't make the same mistake I did. Stay away from those young ones."

I winced. Debated. In the end, said only, "Why do you say that?"

"It's a whole different world, Josh. The way they see sex and love and relationships. Like life's a game. I guess I didn't realize how old-fashioned I was. He made me feel young, you know?"

"Yes," I said, feeling as if my insides were made of lead. "I understand that."

"But it was all in my head. Six months later, I came home to find him spit-roasted between two boys who couldn't have been more than twenty."

"Jesus." I shut my eyes, trying to block out the mental image of Rad in that position with anybody but me.

"Honestly, it wasn't even so much that he was fucking around. It was that he didn't even consider including me. And when I mentioned it, you know what he said?"

"No." And I had a feeling I didn't want to know.

"He said nobody my age would have the stamina to keep up with them anyway."

"Ouch."

He laughed. "Yeah. Well, he was probably right, if you want to know the truth."

"We're not that old."

"Ha! Keep telling yourself that."

I wished I could laugh about it, like him, but nothing about the situation seemed funny. "I'm sorry that happened. You didn't deserve that."

"Well," he said, quietly. "Maybe I did."

We talked a bit longer. Small talk, mostly, asking after each other's family's, but it didn't take long to realize we had nothing left to say but goodbye.

And I spent the rest of the afternoon worrying about my stamina.

Two days before Christmas, the next blow fell. Or, more accurately, the devil himself showed up on my doorstep.

"Merry Christmas!" Wren said as he let himself inside. He was gorgeous as ever, his dark eyes wickedly sexy, his cheeks rosy from the cold. He'd brought the biggest poinsettia I'd ever seen, and held a six-pack of beer clenched precariously in one hand. I didn't move to help him. I watched the flowers tickling his face. Weren't poinsettias poisonous? I pictured his face breaking out in hives and managed to smile.

"Merry Christmas to you, too."

"Is Rad home?"

"No. He's in Provo, visiting his grandfather."

"Oh." He set the plant down and turned his smile on me. I'd never known exactly what Rad had said to him to make the blatant sexual advances stop. I only knew that after that one night in October, Wren hadn't been around nearly so often. When we did see him, he was painfully courteous to me and a bit cold toward Rad.

"Listen," he said, holding a beer out to me. "I hate feeling like we can't be friends. Can we just, I don't know, start over?"

I was sure there some old adage about never trusting the devil, but I foolishly said, "I suppose."

It started out fine. Awkward and painful, but not as bad as a root canal. Unfortunately, somewhere around beer number three, Wren asked the worst question ever.

"So, what'd you get Rad for Christmas?"

"Uh…" An engagement ring, but I was reluctant to tell him.

"You better have something good. He'll go on all day about how the holiday is a corrupted pagan ritual, bastardized by the church, monetized and commercialized by the capitalist system, blah, blah, blah. But I'll tell you what, he's a sucker for Christmas morning. You better believe he's going to bat those big green eyes at you and hope for magic and rainbows."

"Really?"

"Yeah. Really. So, what'd you get him?"

"Well. Um. Jewelry."

"What?" he asked, laughing in disgusted delight. "Jewelry? Are you kidding?" And then, a split second later, the smile fell from his face. "Holy shit."

"What?"

"You're going to propose."

"No!"

Yes.

Maybe.

He shook his head. "No. Dude." He kept shaking his head emphatically. "No. Terrible idea. He'll freak. And not in a good way."

"How do you know?"

"Because he hates stuff like that. Just ask him. He thinks marriage is an outdated notion. A patriarchal plot or some damn thing, thrust on us by the religious overlords or—"

"Excuse me?"

He waved his hand at me. "I don't know, man. All that neo-philosophical bullshit. It goes in one ear and out the other, but I'll tell you this much: he doesn't believe in any of it. Marriage. Long-term commitment. Long-term monogamy. None of it."

"But—"

He laughed again, and this time, I heard the note of cruelty in his voice. I heard the disdain he'd managed to hide for so long. Maybe he'd been waiting for this. Maybe it was the beer. Maybe I was finally hearing him clearly for the first time. "Look, Josh. Just because he told me no, just because he's been shacked up with you, playing house, enjoying his little ride on the love boat doesn't mean it's going to last. Rad's a loose cannon. A free spirit, through and through. In the end, he always gets bored. And you know what he does then?"

"No," I said, my throat tight.

Wren grinned at me, and I could have sworn I heard the hounds of hell laughing outside my door. "He comes crawling back to me.

I didn't want to believe Wren, but that night, when Rad came home, I couldn't stop the wheels in my head from spinning. I couldn't stop the flood of images — Rad leaving me, Rad cheating on me, Rad telling me I didn't have enough stamina. Rad telling me Wren was the one he loved.

I was mixed up, half drunk and half hung over, and already, my plans for Christmas seemed like a fool's notion.

I'd take Rad to Tower Arch, and we'd stand there shivering, freezing our asses off until sunset, and then I'd take out the ring. I'd get down on my knee. And Rad would freak, exactly like Wren had said. He'd tell me to get up. To take back the ring. To stop acting like an old-fashioned idiot. He'd tell me that marriage was a lie and a sham and a god damn stupid idea. And then we'd come back home, and I'd have to smile and pretend like he hadn't broken my heart.

Or maybe I'd have to move out.

Where would I go? Back to San Diego, to the condo I'd once shared with Roger? To Oregon, where I'd first met Rad? To the living room where we'd fucked like sex-crazed lunatics on the hardwood floor, and the bedroom where we'd first made love? The kitchen we'd sat in when he asked me to come and visit for as long as it felt like an adventure?

Was this still an adventure?

Had it ever been one for him?

What was I doing here? How could I let four and a half meager months of passion and sex and laughter and love — yes, god damn it, love! — lead me into thinking I should propose?

Maybe I should wait. After all, it didn't have to be now. I could hang onto the ring. See how I felt about it when Valentine's Day rolled around. But why? Why make it harder on myself, when I knew it'd only end with me broken and lost and saying goodbye?

"What's going on with you?" Rad asked me on Christmas Eve, as we left the restaurant, where I'd sat watching the others laugh and be merry, feeling as if my heart were a million miles away.

"Do you like Christmas?"

"What?"

"You heard me. Do you like Christmas?" Sure he'd let me put up a tiny little tree in the corner of the living room, laughing at me as I did it. Sure, he'd smiled when I'd hung stockings off the air-conditioning unit. But Wren's words haunted me.

"Well." He hooked his arm in mine as we walked slowly toward my car. "The original pagan yule celebrations have been completely bastardized by the Christians, and even that's been corrupted beyond belief by the commercialism of—"

"Do you think marriage is an outdated notion? And long-term commitment?"

"Absolutely. I mean, most cultural anthropologists agree that marriage is mostly a social tool used to control the masses. Joining two free selves into one only serves to deny the freedom of each individual, right?"

"Right," I said, wondering how I could feel so miserable and so lost on this, of all nights.

"It's basically a government-sanctioned form of oppression."

"Of course."

"Oh my god, I forgot to get a present for Yashe. We have to stop at the grocery store for a bone or something."

"You bet."

But the world had never seemed darker to me, and that night, lying in bed, I realized it was time for me to leave. I'd had my fun. I'd pretended I could be young. I'd reveled in his energy and his freshness and his off-beat ways. But he was full of youth and life and spirit, and I was relic of some other age. He didn't want to be tied down, and I didn't want to spend another day falling deeper in love with a man who would only reject me in the end.

I tossed and turned all night, playing it out in my mind. As the minutes ticked past, my options seemed to dwindle down to one heartbreaking possibility.

At four o'clock, I rolled quietly out of bed. My duffel bag lay buried beneath a pile of shoes and gloves at the bottom of the coat closet. I half hoped he'd wake as I stuffed a few things into it, including the ring I never should have bought, but he didn't. He slept peacefully.

Finally, with a heavy lump in my throat and nothing left to do but walk out the door, I stopped by the side of the bed.

I studied him, trying desperately to memorize every line of his face. Every tangled curl of his hair. Remembering the taste of him, and the way he felt in my arms. Hearing his laughter echoing in my ears.

God, I loved him, but it was time to say goodbye. I didn't dare wake him. I left a note instead.

> *Rad—*
>
> *I hate to leave like this, and on Christmas too, but I think it's time. I've worn out my welcome. You're young, and you don't want to be stuck with an old man like me. These last few months have been the greatest of my life. I'll never forget you.*
>
> *Thanks for the adventure.*
> *All my love-*
> *Josh*

And then I cried all the way to the Moab airport.

Chapter Seven

I arrived at the airport at five am, and had to wait until six for it to open. The building wasn't much bigger than a one-car garage. The poor employee doomed to work on Christmas Day informed me that the only flight out wasn't until ten. I was surprised to learn it was nearly full, but I was able to get a ticket. She sent me through security to the terminal, if it could be called that. It had one podium. One gate. A vending machine. Maybe thirty seats. I took one and waited as the small building filled around me. I didn't look around. I didn't want to know if any of these people were ones I'd come to call friends. I didn't want to face anybody with my eyes still red and swollen and the tiny ring like an albatross in my bag.

Some part of me screamed that I was making the wrong decision. That I was being a complete fool, sneaking out like this on Christmas Day. In the cold light of morning, my note felt juvenile. My entire thought process felt backward, like a child throwing a tantrum. I didn't want to leave, but I couldn't stand the thought of driving back. Of facing Rad. Of telling him that I'd only had one plan for Christmas Day, but I'd realized too late it was a mistake.

"Josh!"

I jumped out of my seat. Every person in the tiny airport turned toward Rad, who stood in the doorway, his hair a wild mess around his head, his coat thrown on over sweats and a Left Hand Brewery T-shirt that had more holes than fabric.

He'd stopped to put on his hiking boots, though.

"How'd you get through security?"

"I had to buy a god damn ticket!"

"But, what are you doing here?"

"Are you fucking kidding me? I thought you'd gone out for coffee or donuts or something. And then you never came back, and I finally start looking around, and I find *this*?" He held up the note I'd left.

"I'm sorry," I said, moving toward him in the small space, away from the other passengers, as if we could find some privacy in the small, cramped building. "I should have waited until you were awake, but I didn't think I could bear to face you. I didn't think I could say what I needed to say."

"So you leave me a god damn note?" He wadded it up and threw it at me. It bounced off my chest and rolled under the seat of a woman who was pointedly studying the ceiling. "I can't believe you'd do this to me!"

"I'm sorry. I should have—"

"I don't understand. I thought we were doing so well. I thought everything was perfect. I thought…" His voice broke. He swallowed hard. Was he fighting tears? "I thought you loved me."

"I do." And god, it hurt to say it this way, to finally utter those words for the first time, not in some glorious place like I'd envisioned, but in the middle of the airport, surrounded by strangers, feeling like the world was falling apart around me. "God, *I do*. But I'm not what you want. I'm not the kind of person you really want to be with."

"Is that what you think?"

"It's what I know."

"And do I get any say in that? Or are you just going to take your own word for it?"

I sighed, glancing around at the crowded airport, and the other holiday travelers who were staring fixedly at some distant point as they eavesdropped on our conversation. "I talked to Wren—"

"Wren? You talked to *Wren*? About *us*? And you actually listened to him? Jesus, Josh, you're such an idiot sometimes! How could you possibly take Wren's word when it comes to our relationship?"

"You're right," I conceded. "I didn't want to listen to him, but then I asked you."

He blinked at me in confusion. "You asked me what? When? I don't remember you asking if I wanted to break up, or if you were the kind of guy I wanted to be with. I sure as hell don't remember telling you that I wanted you to leave!"

"I asked if you thought marriage and long-term commitment were outdated ideas, and you said yes."

"That's because they *are* outdated ideas. So what? So are CDs, and I still buy those!"

Now it was my turn to be confused. "CDs are outdated?"

"Of course they are!"

"Then how am I supposed to buy music?"

"MP3s, for fuck sake!"

"I just finished replacing all my cassettes."

"Jesus, Josh. I'm standing here trying to tell you that I love you, and you're worried about your cassette tapes?"

"Wait. *What?*"

"And you're going to leave just because I said marriage is outdated? Why? What the hell does that have to do with—" His eyes widened in a way that might have been comical at some other point in time. "Were you planning to propose?"

"Did you just say you love me?"

"Stop changing the subject!"

I might have argued that he was the one changing the subject, but I let it go. I was torn between frustration and the irresistible urge to laugh. He was impossible, yes. And yet, wasn't this exactly why I wanted to marry him? Because he made me crazy in the best possible way? "Yes," I said quietly. "I was going to propose."

He put both hands over his lips, as if trying to hold something in. "Oh my god."

"But then Wren made this big stink, and when I asked you—"

"Is there a ring?"

"What?"

"Did you buy me a ring?"

"I... Yeah." But I was still hung up on what he'd said before. "Do you really love me?"

He blinked at me, his fingers still covering his lips, and a laugh bubbled out of him. Not mirth, exactly, but exasperation and confusion and heartbreak all rolled into one achingly beautiful sound. "You really have to ask me that? I'm standing here making a complete ass out of myself in the middle of the god damn airport on Christmas Day just to keep you from leaving me, and you have to ask me whether or not I love you?"

"Yes."

He closed his eyes and took a deep breath. He dropped his hands, squared his shoulders as if preparing for battle, and finally met my gaze. "I do. Even though you're being the world's biggest jackass right now. And I'm furious that you'd listen to Wren instead of talking to me, and that you'd leave me with nothing but a god damn note. But yes, I love you more than anything, partly because you're so unbelievably clueless."

My world spun. Whispers buzzed around me. Quiet chuckles reached my ears from people no longer bothering to pretend they weren't listening, but all I could see was him. I wasn't sure what to say first. That I loved him too, or that I didn't really want to go, or that I truly was the world's biggest idiot for letting Wren sow doubt in my heart. But Rad spoke again before I figured out what to say.

"Can I see the ring?"

"What?"

"Do you still have the ring?"

And then, I understood. I dropped my duffel to the floor and knelt beside it to dig through its contents. I stood up and held the little box out to him.

He blinked at me, his expression somewhere between exasperation and anger and amusement. "Not like that! Do it right. Do it the way you planned to do it."

"Well, I planned to take you up to Tower Arch, right at sunset."

"Oh my god," he said again. He blinked, and tears brimmed in his eyes again, but he wiped them hurriedly away. "Okay. I can let that part go. It would've been cold as hell anyway. But then what? You were just going to shove that stupid box at me and hope for the best?"

I fought back a laugh. "No."

"Then do it right," he said, waving his hands at me in angry exasperation. "Do what you planned. Say what you were going to say!"

And in that moment, I loved him more than ever. I loved that he could make me feel like such a fool while still making me feel like he loved me.

And yes, he really did love me. How I'd ever doubted it, I didn't know, but at least he'd said it now. And he was right. He deserved more than me pushing a ring at him. I'd lost out on my visions of proposing in the blinding brilliance of the setting sun, but I could at least give him this.

I'd worried that I'd be nervous when the time came to actually propose, but now, after everything that had happened, I wasn't scared at all. I opened the box so he could see the simple silver ring inside. The crowd, now standing in a blatant circle around us, watching the entire spectacle, murmured and began to smile. I did my best to ignore them. I got down on my knee and looked up into his eyes.

"Radcliffe Fox, these last few months with you have been the greatest adventure of my life, and I don't ever want that adventure to end. I love you, and the only thing I want for Christmas is for you to say you'll be my husband. Will you marry me?"

He put his shaking fingers over his lips again. For a moment he stood frozen, as if simply soaking it all in, but then he nodded. "Yes," he said in a whisper. "Yes, I'll marry you."

A curious buzz ran through the crowd. They hadn't heard his answer. But when I stood up and he threw himself into my arms, they figured it out. They cheered. They clapped. And all I could think as I held Rad close was how I'd ruined everything.

"I'm sorry," I told him. "I'm sorry I messed it up. I'm sorry I'm so stupid. I'd hoped to give you a wonderful moment that you'd never forget, but—"

He broke away from me, laughing. He glanced around at the dispersing crowd, some of whom were calling out congratulations before they left. "Are you kidding? You think I could ever forget this?"

"This wasn't what I had in mind."

"But it's wonderful anyway." He pulled me close and kissed me. "It's perfect."

"Really?"

"It's like digging up your floor, all over again."

I smiled, remembering. "That was one of the greatest moments of my life."

"And this one?"

"It definitely makes the short list."

"Mine too." He took my hand. "So now that's settled, are you ready to come home?"

"Absolutely."

"Can we stop for breakfast on the way? Some asshole never showed up with my donut, and now I'm starving."

I laughed. "Anything you want."

"Good." He took my hand and led me toward the door, and the blazing sunlight of Christmas Day. "By the way…"

"Yeah?"

"You're reimbursing me for that ticket."

It was a small price to pay for the adventure of a lifetime.

One More Soldier

I first met Bran eight years ago. He was eleven years old. I was twenty-eight.

It was 1963 and I had just returned home from a long day fixing cars. It was an excruciatingly hot Houston day. The garage I worked at had been even hotter.

Coming home wasn't much of a relief. My apartment didn't have air conditioning and it was like an oven, as usual. I wolfed downed two PB&Js and a beer, smoked a nice fat bowl, and then put on my swimming suit and headed for the pool. My apartment complex was made up of three buildings that formed a horseshoe around a large community pool, and I couldn't wait to immerse myself in the relatively cool water. It was how I passed most of my evenings in the summer. I'd spend twenty to forty minutes floating blissfully on the surface while my high wore off and then do a few laps before dragging myself off to bed to get up at six the next morning.

I arrived at the pool a little after eight, hoping I'd have it to myself. As far as I was concerned that was the benefit of coming to the pool late. But this time I found a kid I'd never seen before sitting on the edge with his feet dangling in.

"Hiya mister!" he said as I came through the gate.

I groaned mentally. Sharing the pool with kids was the worst. They were always screaming and splashing when all I wanted was a little bit of silent relaxation. But I said, "Hey."

"I'm Brannon Nelson," he said. "What's your name?"

"Will."

"What's your last name? My ma says I have to call grown-ups by their last name."

"Constantinescu."

"Constantil . . . ?" he trailed away uncertainly.

I sighed, wishing not for the first time my father's father had done what other immigrants had chosen to do and

Americanized his name. But no such luck for me. "Forget it, kid," I said. "Just call me Will."

"Okay." He was skinny and pale and his dark blonde hair was cropped short. He was in that terribly awkward pre-adolescent stage where he seemed to be nothing but big teeth, protuberant ears, and giant feet. "My ma and I just moved into apartment twelve—"

"That's great, kid," I said, hoping to quell the story of his life, which I had a feeling he was just dying to share. As if to prove me right he kept talking as if I hadn't spoken at all.

"—in building C. My sister, too, but she's only eight. She wanted to come to the pool with me but my ma said no, she's too little, and it's almost her bedtime anyway, but since I'm eleven I can stay out later so she said I could come check out the pool, and it's really swell, isn't it? I mean, we never had a pool before! But I bet it's gonna be lots of fun. We used to live—"

Holy hell, this was going to be worse than I thought. I dove into the pool and was able to swim in underwater silence to the other edge before surfacing next to him. He was still talking.

"—died last year. I guess really, it was more like two years ago now, just about, and we stayed there for a while, but then my ma said we couldn't afford to live there no more so we moved here. She works at the diner down the street you know, so she says this is perfect 'cause it's so close, and I have to watch my sister until my ma gets home, but that's usually around seven, and after that she says I can come to the pool and—"

"Jesus, kid," I said in exacerbation, "shut up for half a second, will you?"

"Sure," he said.

And to my surprise, he did. He just sat there smiling at me, not saying a word. I was a little taken aback by his acquiescence. "Okay then," I said awkwardly. "Just gimme a few minutes, before you start talking again."

"Sure thing, mister."

I didn't actually expect him to be quiet for long, but I'd take what I could get. I stretched out on my back, closed my eyes, and let myself drift on the surface, riding out the peak of my high, letting my mind turn off and my body cool down, until I finally emerged into the mellow THC-induced valley below that would carry me through until bedtime. I slowly cracked my eyelids open and looked over at him. He was still sitting in the same spot, watching me.

"Thanks, kid."

"Sure thing, mister."

"It's Will."

"Okay, Will."

"How'd your dad die?"

"In a car wreck."

"Jeez, I'm sorry, kid. That sucks."

"I know." He said it in a matter-of-fact tone that was way too old for his eleven years and it threw me a bit.

"Are you going to get in?" I asked. "Or are you just going to sit there all night?"

"Can't swim."

"Are you serious?"

"Ma says maybe she can afford lessons next year."

It was bad enough to live in the Houston heat. Now he had access to a pool but wouldn't be able to use it? That'd be tough on an adult, but it had to be absolute torture for a kid his age. "Come on, kid," I said, before I had time to think about what a bad idea it was. "I'll teach you."

So for better or worse, I ended up teaching Brannon to swim. He met me the next three nights at the pool. He was a quick learner and not even bad company, for a kid. But on Friday night, I told him I wouldn't be there the next evening. I could tell he was disappointed, but it didn't matter. I sure as hell wasn't going to change my mind. Saturday was my night for myself, when I would sneak off to one of the little-known bars downtown for guys like me—guys who preferred other guys. I never brought anybody home, but that one night each week I allowed myself the release of actually being touched by another man. Whether it was following one to his place or just a quick fuck in the back room of the bar, it was something, and I wasn't about to give it up for some kid.

"I can still meet you on Sunday," I told him.

"I can't swim on Sundays," he said. "Ma says it's the Sabbath. I think when God said you shouldn't work on the Sabbath he didn't mean swimming, but ma says it's inappropriate."

I wasn't sure whether God cared about swimming or not, but I sure as hell wasn't going to contradict any kid's mom. "Then I'll see you Monday."

He followed me around for the rest of the summer, which just about drove me nuts, but once school started in the fall he found friends his own age.

Still, I would see him once or twice a month, at the pool or in the laundry room. He brought in my mail when I left town to visit my folks. He came to me when he needed help with his homework, or when his mom pissed him off. Sometimes he got on my nerves, but mostly I could tolerate him. He was a smart kid and he'd talk your ear off of if you let him. More than once I snapped and told him to shut the hell up. But just like that first day at the pool, he took it in stride.

The one good thing about a kid his age was that he never asked any of the questions: Why wasn't I seeing anyone? At the ripe old age of twenty-eight, why hadn't I settled down and gotten married? Was I going to stay a bachelor forever? Didn't I want a nice woman to take care of me? They were questions adults always seemed to feel they were justified in asking. I thought maybe they could have learned a lot from Bran.

Over the next few years, I watched him grow. He was still skinny and awkward and gangly, although he did finally grow into his feet. He played basketball at his high school and he was incredibly bright and inquisitive.

In 1967 Timothy Leary got everybody buzzing about "questioning authority". Sometimes I thought Bran took the advice a bit too much to heart, but it was purely academic for him. He was much less rebellious than I had been at his age.

Early in his sophomore year of high school we realized I could no longer help him with his homework. He was so much smarter than I had ever been, and the string of numbers and letters he put in front of me was well beyond my ability. It embarrassed me, but he didn't seem to hold it against me.

I'd always been a fuck-up. I'd finished high school, but only barely. I spent the first few years after graduation pumping gas, until my boss Ed took me under his wing and taught me how to fix cars. It was a living, but it sure wasn't my dream. I knew Bran had potential, and I hoped he would be wiser than I had been. I tried to talk him into going to college, but he always shrugged me off. I was disappointed when, the summer before his senior year, he informed me that he had dropped out of school.

"Bran, you could have gone to college!" I said in frustration. "Why would you drop out now?"

It was a Wednesday night deep in August of 1969 and the heat seemed to lie like a blanket across the city, weighing us all down. Even the tepid water of the swimming pool could do little to cool us off.

"The rent keeps going up, and my ma's tips don't," he said defensively. "I can't expect her to continue supporting me, Will. I'm old enough to support myself."

I hated the thought of him wasting his intelligence, becoming a flunky like me, but what could I say? "What will you do?" I asked.

"I got a job on a ranch over near San Antonio. Room and board provided."

"Ranching's hard work," I said, but he just shrugged.

"I can handle it, and it pays good."

"When do you leave?"

"My ma's driving me out there tomorrow."

There wasn't much left to say after that. We swam a little longer, dunking each other and horseplaying as if we were both kids, rather than one of us being in his thirties. But finally it was time to go.

"Hey Will?" he said as we were about to part ways at the gate. "Thanks, man."

"For what?"

He shrugged, clearly embarrassed. "For always being here when I needed you."

Other than teaching him to swim six years earlier, I didn't really feel like I'd done much for him. But his face was full of nervous sincerity, and so I said, "No problem, kid." He looked a bit perturbed at still being referred to as a kid, which made me laugh. "Take care of yourself, Bran."

"You too."

The months passed for me as they always did. The scorching heat of summer dwindled into winter. Since Bran wasn't around that year, I had his sister Janice bring in my mail while I was visiting my parents over Christmas. Janice told me Bran had been home for the holiday, but he was gone again by the time I returned home.

I had a casual affair that year with a married man named Frank. It started in the fall and lasted through the spring. He would call me whenever his wife was out of town and we'd spend a few hours together at his house. It wasn't anything like a real relationship. Not that I'd ever *had* a real relationship. Still, I figured it was the best two gay men could hope for, even if it did involve sneaking around and keeping secrets. But in June of 1970 his wife confronted him, demanding to know if he was having an affair. He confessed he was, although he didn't ever admit that it was with another man, and they left town. I never heard from him again. I hated having to go back to the bars to get laid, but other than that, there was nothing about our relationship worth mourning.

One hot summer evening in July found me at the pool, waiting for the heat of day to pass so that I could return to my apartment. At thirty-five I was finding it more difficult to keep myself in shape than when I was in my twenties. Even the hard labor at the garage wasn't enough to keep the love handles at bay. I spent a lot more of my pool time doing laps than floating now.

When I finished I was surprised to find that I was no longer alone. I had been so engrossed in my workout I hadn't noticed the newcomer entering the fenced-in pool area. I definitely noticed now though. He was hard to miss. The man's back was to me and he was wearing only short, tight swim trunks. The pool wasn't well lit, but he was standing directly under one of the lamps and I could see that his body was deeply tanned and heavily muscled. Whoever it was, I was pretty damn sure I hadn't seen him around the apartments before. And I was praying to whatever God might be listening that he was gay.

And then he turned around and said happily, "Hey Will! How've you been?"

My stunned brain took a minute to connect that voice to a known person in my head. "Bran?" I asked in surprise.

"You didn't recognize me?"

"No," I said, and he laughed.

"The light's not that good out here."

That was true, but the real reason I hadn't recognized him was that he was an entirely different person now. My memory of him was of a skinny, awkward kid. He most definitely wasn't that any more. His arms and chest were muscular, his stomach ridged. The dark blonde hair that had always been shaved short was now hanging in his eyes and was sun-bleached platinum. I hadn't seen him since the summer before, and in that year he had definitely become a man. A very fine man at that. I was torn between wanting to look at every inch of him and feeling like a pedophile for even thinking of looking.

"I've been working at that ranch the past year," he said as he slid gracefully into the pool. "But I decided to come home for a bit."

"That's great, kid," I said, because it was the only thing I could think of to say. He sank up to his chin and started to swim toward where I stood in the chest-deep water. "So you'll be here for the summer?" I asked.

"Not that long," he said. He was only a few feet away from me now, swimming steadily. In the low light, I saw just a flash of teeth as he grinned at me. And then his head went under, and he kicked his feet up, propelling himself down under the surface of the water. I knew it was coming, but I didn't move fast enough. He grabbed my knees from below and pulled my feet out from under me, pulling me under.

When I surfaced, sputtering and coughing water, he was laughing. "You used to do that to me every chance you got," he said.

"I guess you did owe me."

His grin got bigger. "We're not even yet, Will." He lunged at me, launching himself up out of the water and coming down with his hands on my shoulders, pushing me under again. It was a classic move -- every boy in the world and probably most of the girls too, had dunked somebody in exactly that same way at one time or another. I was more prepared for it this time and got a good lung full of air before he pushed me down. He was still laughing when I came back up.

"Is this some kind of challenge?" I joked.

Bran laughed. "Exactly."

The word was barely out of his mouth before I jumped at him, pushing him under as he had done to me. He came up laughing. "Is that all you've got, old man?"

"Oh, you're in trouble now!" I was laughing too as I pushed him under. He didn't resist much, and this time he stayed under. I knew he was going to try to grab my legs again, but in the low light I couldn't see below the surface enough to know which side he was coming from.

He ended up hitting me from the left. One of his arms hit me behind the knees, folding my legs underneath me. And his other hand . . . his other hand landed right on my groin as he pushed me down. It wasn't a hard impact. It was gentle, almost exploring.

I pushed away from him hard and came up sputtering. He was laughing again and I wished I could see his face. I wanted to see if he was embarrassed, or oblivious, or . . .

"We're still not even, Will." The low suggestive timbre of his voice hit me.

That contact had *not* been accidental.

My body responded against my will, and I was horrified. This was Bran! I had known him since he was only eleven, skinny and fighting acne. I had taught him to swim. I had helped him with his math homework. I had played with him in this pool more times than I could count, dunking him as he had just done to me . . . Well. Not *exactly* as he had just done to me.

He started to move closer again, and I found myself backing up. "I have to go," I said shakily.

His progress toward me stopped. "Sure thing, Will." The disappointment in his voice was obvious.

I scrambled out of the pool quickly and grabbed my towel, thankful that between it and the low light he couldn't see the effect his touch had on me. I hated that I was aroused at all. I felt unclean. Like a pervert.

I didn't look back as I left the pool. I didn't even say goodbye.

Once I was back in the comfort of my own apartment, I took a shower. A very fast, very cold shower. Normally the shower after a swim might have included masturbating, but I wasn't about to allow myself any such indulgence after what had just happened. It felt wrong.

I got into bed and lay there, wide awake, replaying the incident in my mind. Had I imagined it? Certainly I hadn't imagined the hand on my groin. But my surety it had been deliberate? As I thought it over more I decided I had overreacted. First of all, I had never had any indication that he was gay. Of course, it wasn't as if I had ever talked to him about it. And I hadn't known him all that well. After all, he had only been a kid. Still, it seemed unlikely. Then there was the fact that I was seventeen years older than him. I wasn't in bad shape for my age, but he was young, and gorgeous. Why would he waste his time hitting on me? I was only a couple of years younger than his *mother*!

I hadn't been able to see his expression at the pool. My momentary conviction that he was making an advance was based on nothing more than his voice. And he had only said five words.

It was ridiculous. I was being a fool. In hindsight I regretted my hasty retreat from the pool. No doubt if I had stayed my suspicions would have been proven groundless.

I breathed a sigh of relief, feeling like my world made sense once again. And I finally fell asleep.

The next evening he showed up at the pool as I was finishing my laps again. This time there was no horseplay. He kept his distance, talking nonstop about his job at the farm. As we chatted casually, my belief the contact had been accidental seemed to be confirmed. I felt silly for having ever believed he'd been coming on to me.

"I really have to go," I finally told him as I got out of the pool and started to dry off. "I have to be at work early tomorrow."

"Will? Can I ask you a favor?"

"Sure."

"I bought a used stereo outta the paper. Got it all the way home and realized I got no clue how to set it up. Think you could help me with it?"

"You bet. Probably not tomorrow, but I could come by Saturday morning. Around ten?"

"That'd be great," he said. "Thanks."

"No problem." He was in the deep end of the pool, apparently treading water. Looking out at him in the near-dark, he was barely more than a shadow. It was easy to remember him as the scrawny teenager he had been the summer before. "Goodnight, Bran."

"Goodnight," he said. I turned to leave the pool area, but just as I was opening the gate, he called out, "Hey Will?"

"Yeah?"

It took him a second. I waited, one hand on the open gate, and finally he said, "I'm eighteen now you know." And just like that, my whole world flipped upside down. "See you Saturday."

Bran's pointed statement about his age was not lost on me. There was only one reason he would feel the need to tell me his age, and that one reason was the most wrong reason I could think of. I avoided the pool on Friday night, but I had promised to help him with his stereo on Saturday. I debating not going, but I knew he would only seek me out. In the end it seemed safer to go to his house and hope the presence of his mother or sister would deter his advances.

His mom wasn't at the apartment when I arrived, but his sister Janice let me in the front door. She waved me dismissively toward his room before resuming her chattering phone conversation.

Bran wasn't in his room, but the stereo equipment was stacked on a desk and I groaned when I saw it. Miles of speaker wire hung in a tangled mess from the back of each piece. Whoever owned it before Bran had obviously done the bare minimum amount of work necessary, unhooking just enough wires to allow Bran to pull the components out of the cabinet. I'd have to untangle the whole rat's nest before I could even start to hook it up.

"What a mess, huh?" Brannon said behind me.

"It's a disaster. What the hell were they—" I turned to face him, and whatever words I might have had to say after that disappeared at the sight of him.

He was breathtaking.

Bran had obviously just come from the shower. Water dripped from his hair, beading on his strong, broad shoulders. He wore only a towel. Above it, his stomach was smooth and flat. Below it, his legs were strong and shapely.

"Yes?" he asked jokingly, interrupting my rather too-erotic thoughts.

I jerked my eyes away from his legs and up to his face. He grinned at me mischievously, and I turned my back on him as quickly as I could. *Steady, Will*, I chastised myself mentally. *Just get the damn stereo hooked up and get the hell out of here.* "What were they thinking?" I asked shakily.

"I think they were in a hurry to get rid of it and put their new one in," he said. A drawer opened and closed behind me. I risked a glance over my shoulder. His back was to me. He had dropped his towel and was bending over to step into a pair of shorts. Although his back was tanned a deep, dark brown, his ass was pale white, his cheeks incredibly round and muscular.

I averted my eyes again, closing them tight and trying to think about baseball. Or stereo equipment. Or . . .

"Is everything all right, Will?"

"Sure." But everything was *not* all right. There was something very wrong with my voice. It was decidedly too high. And too shaky.

"Do you want me to try to help, or should I just stay out of your way?"

"Ummm . . ." I opened my eyes again and looked back at him. He had donned a pair of shorts, and there really was no other word for them. Shorts. *Short* shorts. Once upon a time, they had possibly been a pair of sweat pants, but he had cut the legs off of them. And once upon a time they had probably fit him. But now they were more than a bit too small. The shorts had been washed so many times the fabric seemed impossibly thin. It was stretched tight and did nothing to disguise the outline of what was underneath them. The hem of the cut-off legs curled up revealing the curve at the top of his thigh, where it dipped toward—

Lord help me! "Just stay over there," I snapped, turning away, and I knew it came out sounding much angrier than I had intended.

"Okay," he said, sounding disappointed.

I didn't care. I didn't care if he was hurt, or disappointed, or angry. I didn't care if he was confused. I only cared about one thing: getting the fuck out of there before my brain turned off and allowed the turned-on part of my body to take over.

I started pulling at cords, resisting the urge to take out my frustration on them by simply ripping them away from the stereo. I started at the top piece and began to systematically unhook the various cables from the components. It didn't take long, thank goodness. Only a few minutes. Then another few minutes while I untangled them all. Then a few more as I started reconnecting them. It was completely silent in the room all the while. But I could feel him behind me, watching me.

I tried not to think about those damn shorts he was wearing.

I failed.

"Almost there," I said. That wasn't entirely true, but I felt like I needed to say something to break the silence.

"There's no hurry." I could tell without looking that he was now right behind me. Maybe less than a foot away.

"I just . . . I have to . . ." *Christ, what did I have to do?* "Once I connect this last cable, it should work."

"Great," he said, and he was even closer now.

My shaking hands made the job more difficult than it should have been, but I finally got the last component hooked up. "All done!" I announced. I stood up and hit the power button.

Nothing happened.

Shit.

"It's not working," he said, and good lord, how could he be so close? It sounded like he was almost on top of me -- and the thoughts that brought to mind were completely inappropriate. I resisted the urge to turn around and look at him. That wouldn't help anything!

I leaned over the top of the stereo again, studying the cables emerging from the back of it. I couldn't think straight. My heart was pounding. Why wouldn't the God damn thing just turn on so I could get out of Bran's room? What had I missed?

And then he touched me.

It wasn't much. Just his hand, light and hesitant on the small of my back, but my entire world suddenly disappeared. My entire awareness shrank to that one point of contact. I had to force myself to breathe.

"Will?" he asked quietly, his voice barely a whisper.

Oh God, this can't be happening. How am I supposed to handle this? I had no idea, but what I told myself was, *Act casual!* "I'm not sure why it's not working," I said, and I couldn't believe how much my voice shook.

"Don't worry about it." And then he took that last tiny step toward me. I couldn't see him, but I felt it when his groin, and there could be no doubt that he was completely erect, pushed against my ass.

I froze. I didn't even breathe. Every part of me was stone still, except the traitorous villain in my pants. He shifted in a way that was entirely wrong. Or right. Depending on how you looked at it.

"I think I should go," I managed to say, but he didn't move out from behind me. In fact, he pressed closer. I felt his weight against my back and his lips against my neck.

"Please don't, Will," he whispered. His hand slid across my stomach, and my breath caught in my throat. He pushed harder against me and his hand started inching toward my groin.

"Bran," I made myself say, even though my body screamed for me to stop thinking and start reacting, "this is wrong on so many levels."

"I'm not a kid anymore," he said softly. And then his hand moved down, cupping my growing erection through my jeans. I heard myself groan. "*Please*," he whispered hoarsely, "don't say no."

I took a deep breath, fighting back the desire burning in the pit of my stomach. I turned to face him, and he backed up, just a bit. Still, he was so very close. We were almost exactly the same height, and I found myself staring into eyes the color of storm clouds. My erection strained at the zipper on my jeans, and my mind raced with thoughts of what it would feel like to kiss him. My eyes traveled down his tan, muscular body to the thin fabric of his shorts, stretched even tighter now over his erect cock. A tiny wet spot was forming on the fabric where his tip pushed toward the waistband. I thought about how easy it would be to hook my fingers into that elastic and pull his shorts out of the way. I imagined sinking to my knees in front of him, feeling the weight of his cock against my tongue, tasting that little drop of saltiness in the back of my throat. I imagined his hands gripping my head, pulling me down his length.

"Oh Jesus," I moaned, closing my eyes tight.

"Will?" he asked quietly, and I felt him move closer. I felt his hands pulling me against him, and that tempting bulge pushing against my own. I felt his breath on my cheek and then his lips against my ear. "Please let me touch you," he whispered. But the voice I heard was the voice of the boy in my memory, young and gangly, and it horrified me.

"I can't do this!" I said, pushing him away. "I can't!" I turned and fled his room, practically running, and nearly knocking his sister over in my hurry to get out the front door.

"Will, wait," I heard him call, but I sure as hell didn't stop.

Upon reaching the safety of my own apartment I slammed the door shut and leaned against it as if I had to hold the entire world at bay.

What now?

There was a terrible tightness in my groin, the almost painful feeling of having been so close and yet finding no release. I couldn't get him out of my head: the sight of his erection straining against the fabric of his shorts, the feel of his hands pulling me close, the sound of his voice in my ear, whispering "*Please let me touch you.*"

I ripped my pants open and grabbed my still erect cock, determined to grant myself some type of relief. But then came the memory of him as a kid, only seven years ago, gangly and awkward, sitting on the side of the pool, saying, "*Hiya mister!*"

I stopped short, feeling sick to my stomach and terribly unclean.

A cold shower. That was what I needed. A cold shower, and a beer. Or maybe a six-pack. It was Saturday and I didn't have to work the next day. Normally Saturday night meant going to the bar and getting laid, but I wasn't sure I could face it. I wasn't sure I would be able to keep my mind from straying to him, to Bran.

Why me? That was the thought that kept going around and around in my head. Why me? Bran was eighteen, built, and completely gorgeous. He could go to a bar downtown and pick up the man of his choice in a matter of minutes. So why in the world would he want a thirty-five year old mechanic like me?

I was still leaning against the door when he knocked, and I jumped half out of my skin.

"Will?" he called out. "Are you in there?"

"*NO!*"

"Can I come in?"

"That's definitely not a good idea."

He was quiet for a moment, and then he said, "It wasn't plugged in. That's why it didn't turn on."

It took me half a second to figure out what he was even talking about. *Stereos?* We were talking about stereos? Seriously? "I'm glad you got it figured out."

"Are you really going to make me stand outside?"

"Yes!"

I heard him sigh heavily. "Please, Will. I just want to talk to you."

"That wasn't talking!"

"I know. I . . ." His words trailed away for a moment, and when he resumed, his voice was softer. "I promise to ease up a bit, okay? Just let me in."

"I don't know, Bran . . ."

"I'm not going anywhere, Will," he said, with a hint of laughter in his voice. "You'll have to deal with me eventually."

How many times in my life had I wished a willing partner would come knocking? Now that one had I was afraid to face him. How messed up was that?

I opened the door a crack and peeked out at him. He was still wearing the same shorts, but he had donned a T-shirt too, and I kept my eyes resolutely on his face. "Keep your hands to yourself," I said childishly.

He smiled at me, although it was a sad smile. "I will."

I opened the door and stepped back into the living room, putting as much space between us as I could. He came in, closing the door behind him and leaning against it just as I had done. He was barefoot. He glanced down at my fly, then grinned at me, blushing. "Feel better?"

I glanced down and felt myself blush too as I realized that my pants were still undone.

"No," I snapped as I zipped them.

"I'm sorry if I came on too strong."

"Jesus Christ, Bran. I've known you since you were a kid! Coming on at all is coming on too strong!"

He gazed thoughtfully at the ceiling for a minute. "I didn't realize it would bother you," he said quietly. "Maybe I should have thought of that, but I didn't."

"Bran, you're still a kid—"

"I'm not, Will. I'm eighteen now, and—"

"There are lots of guys out there who'd be thrilled—"

"I don't want them."

"You can't want me, Bran. Not really!"

"There's no time—"

"What do you mean there's no—"

"I've been drafted."

The air seemed to disappear from the room. I felt a terrifying sense of vertigo and I had to close my eyes to keep the room from spinning. "Drafted?" I asked stupidly.

"I leave two weeks from Monday."

Drafted. Sweet little Bran, who didn't know how to swim until he was eleven and finally grew into his feet when he was fifteen and was too damn smart for his own good. It was bad enough that he hadn't gone to college, but now, to be drafted. Sent across the world to that cesspool of a war, possibly to die in the stinking jungle, fighting against the Viet Cong for God knew what.

"Will?" he said quietly, and when I opened my eyes, he was there in front of me, his gray eyes looking into mine. "I have two weeks to live my life, Will. Then it'll be basic training, followed by advanced infantry training, and then I'll start my tour. And that might be it, Will—"

"Don't say that!"

"—we both know I might not make it home--"

"Oh God."

"—and anything I want to do in my life, Will, I have to do it now."

That did at least explain his aggressiveness. Still, I wasn't sure it justified the weakening of my will power. "It doesn't have to be me, Bran. There's a bar downtown. I'll take you there. You can find somebody your own age and--"

A red flush crept up his neck, but he didn't turn away. "I don't want it to be a stranger, Will." He took a step closer. I tried to step back but ran into the wall behind me. "I could do it in the back room of a bar," he said, "or in some guy's car. Or go home with someone I've never met and hope for the best. But those are things I might regret, Will. Not this. Not with you. I know you'll be . . ." He faltered. Swallowed hard. When he continued, his voice was only a whisper. "I know you'll show me what to do."

Suddenly the full extent of what he was asking for hit me. I was surprised at the sense of responsibility it instilled in me. "You've never been with anybody before?"

His cheeks were deep crimson now. "I've fooled around with girls a bit, but," he closed his eyes for a moment, seeming truly embarrassed for the first time. "I couldn't ever . . . you know . . . Make things work." His eyes met mine again. Looking into them, I saw arousal. But there was something like fear in there too.

"This isn't something we can take back, Bran. You have to be sure—"

"I am!" He reached for me, stopping just before his hand reached my hip. My breath caught in my throat anyway, just anticipating. "Let me touch you now, Will. Please."

Right or wrong, my control was slipping. How many times could I say no? "Bran," I said, and my voice didn't even sound like my own. "You're so damn young—"

He quit waiting for me to tell him it was okay. He pushed close and my words died in my throat. One of Bran's arms went around my waist. His other hand slid down my back, between my legs, squeezing, rubbing hard between my cheeks, and I moaned. Oh God, I really did want to give in. He pulled me tight against him.

He leaned close, lightly brushing his lips over mine. "Will," he whispered against my lips. "In less than six months, the US Army will put a gun in my hands and make me a killer. If I'm old enough for that, how can I be too young for this?"

And then he kissed me.

His lips were velvety soft, hesitant and sweet, and I heard myself whimper as the last of my resolve crumbled away. I had no power left to protest. The arms that held me were strong and sure, and the chest I felt beneath my hands definitely belonged to an adult, and any memory I had of the person he had been before fled. Maybe my reasons for saying no had been good, and maybe they hadn't. Either way I could no longer muster any conviction for them. Here and now he was a man in every way, and he wanted me. He *trusted* me.

I wrapped my arms around him and kissed him back, relishing the feel of his hard body against mine. He pressed closer and I let my fingers trail downward, finally touching him through the tantalizingly thin fabric of his shorts. Just the lightest touch of my fingertips, and he gasped, pushing against my hand. His fingers started to fumble at the front of my pants, and I stopped him.

He glanced up at me, startled, and I knew he was afraid I was changing my mind again. The mute plea in his eyes made me smile. "Let's go into the bedroom," I said, and the relief on his face was obvious.

He went ahead of me down the short hallway to my room while I locked my front door. Not that I had any reason to expect people to come busting in, but it seemed prudent. I also stopped in the bathroom for the jar of Vaseline. I wasn't sure we'd get that far but it sure as hell didn't hurt to be prepared.

When I finally made it to my bedroom I found that he'd shed what little clothing he'd been wearing. He was lying naked on my bed, and the view from the door of my room was unbelievably arousing. He lay on his back, his knees bent, his feet flat on the bed. There wasn't much hair on his chest, but his erect cock rested on a large patch of thick, brownish-gold curls. The hair trailed away toward his perineum, and the hint I could see of what was beneath was smooth and hairless. I had every intention of exploring that part of him thoroughly.

But not quite yet.

He watched in nervous anticipation as I undressed. When I was as naked as him I sat across his hips, staring down at him. The Houston heat was starting to permeate my apartment and there was a fine sheen of sweat across his broad chest. Most of my sexual encounters were quick and impersonal. The idea of having an infinite amount of time with him was thrilling, and the realization that every bit of it would be new to him made it even better.

I trailed my fingers down his chest to his navel and heard his breathing speed up in response. My fingers continued downward, following the faint treasure trail to his thick patch of curls. He tried to arch toward my hand, but with my weight across his hips he couldn't move much. He moaned, arousal and frustration fighting for dominance, and I couldn't help but smile. I remembered how it felt to be young and so impatient.

I leaned over and flicked my tongue over his nipple. He still smelled like soap from his shower, his skin was already a little salty. I sucked the sensitive flesh into my mouth and rolled it gently between my lips and he whimpered a little. I moved to the other one, running my tongue in circles around it first, then nipping at it lightly with my teeth.

"Oh God," he moaned, arching against me. His hands made fists in the sheets at his side.

I moved up so I could meet his eyes. "You can tell me to stop anytime," I told him.

He shook his head. "I won't."

"But you can," I stressed. "Anytime."

"Okay."

"Or if you need me to slow down."

"Okay."

I kissed him lightly and felt him tense beneath me. "What's wrong?" I asked.

"Can I touch you now?" he asked.

I laughed before I could stop myself. "I thought we were past that."

He didn't smile back. He looked nervous, but undeniably aroused. "Will you do that again?" he whispered.

I smiled as I moved back down to his nipple. "This?" I asked as I took it in my mouth again, squeezing it between my lips.

"Yesss," he breathed as he grabbed my hair with one hand, pushing himself against me. I increased the pressure, biting just a bit, and the air hissed out between his teeth. "Oh God, I had no idea that could feel so good," he said breathlessly, and I moved to the other side.

I teased him lightly with my tongue for a moment before nipping with my teeth. I bit him harder this time. He gasped, froze for a fraction of a second while that hint of pain turned to pleasure, and then he moaned, low in his throat. Both of his hands gripped my head, pulling me tighter against his chest as I teased his sensitive flesh with my teeth.

He panted hard, grinding his erect cock hard against me, and I might have been able to let him finish just like that but I wanted to give him more. Better to let this wave roll back out to sea than to let it crest so soon. I pulled away and sat up so I could look down at him. His nipples were hard, slightly damp, and bright red against the smooth tan skin of his chest. He was unbelievably gorgeous, his gray eyes needy, begging me for more.

I moved off him, positioning myself so I was lying between his legs, and started to slowly kiss my way from his nipples down to his smooth, flat stomach. He sighed, and his breathing slowed again as he relaxed. When I glanced up at his face his eyes were closed, but there was no doubt in the world that he was enjoying himself. I moved all around the thick curls of his hair, breathing in his heavy, musky scent, kissing him, nipping him. My cheek brushed his cock, and he gasped, straining toward me, his hands clenching the bedsheets at his sides.

I moved lower to his perineum. I caressed him there, first with my fingertip, and then with my tongue. He groaned, a deep sound low in his chest, as I sucked on the thick cord of muscle. I was dying to follow that smooth, pink flesh downward but I stopped myself. *One thing at a time.* This first time needed to be completely for Bran, and that particular area was one he might not be expecting me to touch just yet.

I put my tongue on the root of his cock and slowly, leisurely moved up. I left a wet trail up the loose flesh of his sac to the base of his shaft, then slid even more lazily up to flick my tongue over the sensitive spot just below his slit.

"Will," he hissed. Bran grabbed my head, his hands knotting urgently in my hair.

"Not yet," I told him. I used my fingers to lift his cock so it pointed toward my mouth. I kissed the end of it and felt him shiver from the anticipation. There were salty beads of moisture at the tip and I licked them off before slowly slipping my tongue around his ridge, over and over, making smooth deliberate circles. His calm breathing quickly became ragged, and his moans became whimpers.

"Will," he said again. There was more urgency this time and I knew he was close, far closer than he really wanted to be, but unable to stop the tide that was bearing down on him and I decided I had teased him enough.

I sucked the head of his shaft into my mouth, stopping just below the ridge and sucking hard. He cried out and tensed beneath me. Luckily I knew exactly what he was going to do, even if he didn't. His hands pushed my head down and his hips pushed up. He shoved his cock deep into my throat as he came, his erection pulsing against my tongue. I sucked harder, swallowing fast. I knew exactly how amazing it felt to have your pleasure ripped out of you in just that way.

Bran cried out again, "Oh *God!*"

My own erection was grinding against the bedsheets beneath me and I debated using my hand on it. But only for a moment. It was enough for now to have given something to him.

"Will?" he asked shakily. Bran's hands left my head and I pulled away so I could look up at his face. I thought he would be happy, but instead he seemed worried. "Oh God, Will, I'm so sorry—"

"Why are you sorry?" I asked, quickly moving up so I could look down into his face.

"I don't think I should have . . . while you were . . ."

I managed to keep myself from laughing at his discomfiture although I couldn't stop myself from smiling. "I knew what was going to happen." I saw him relax a bit.

"What about you?" Bran asked, reaching for my cock. I pushed his hand away.

"Later," I said. I leaned down to kiss him and saw the trepidation in his eyes. I moved slowly, giving him plenty of time to stop me. But he didn't.

His reluctance to kiss me after what I had just done only lasted a moment. Once his tongue found mine he moaned again and his arms went around me, holding me tight. He kissed me hard and seemed almost to relish the flavor of his own seed on my tongue.

When I pulled back, I was glad to see that he really was smiling this time. "Holy shit, that was amazing," he said, and I laughed as I rolled off of him. It was getting uncomfortably hot in my room and it was better to lie next to him than on top of him.

We lay there in silence for a while, staring at the ceiling, while he caught his breath. I still couldn't quite believe it was happening. I did my best to keep my mind off the Bran I had known before—and I really did have to separate them very firmly in my mind into two different people: the Bran who was an awkward kid, and the Bran who was very much an adult. An unbelievably sexy adult at that.

I started thinking about earlier in his bedroom—his shorts, and his persistence, and my hasty retreat—and found myself laughing. "Did you really buy that stereo out of the paper?" I asked.

"No," he said, and although I wasn't looking at him I could hear the smile in his voice. "It's mine. Brought it home with me from the ranch and hadn't hooked it up yet. Figured it was as good a way as any to get you into my room."

"Dirty trick, Bran."

He laughed. "Maybe, but it was all I could think of. I've never tried to seduce anyone before."

That made sense. It wasn't as if guys like us had opportunities every day. "How did you know about me?" I asked, because I tried very hard to keep a low profile.

He smiled at me, and a light blush crept up his cheeks. "I was afraid you'd ask me that."

"Why? What do you mean?"

He rolled away from me so he could reach over the edge of the bed to the bottom drawer of my bedside table. The drawer where I kept my magazines. I didn't have many, maybe a dozen dog-eared copies of *Physique Pictorial*, *Young Adonis*, and *Grecian Guild Pictorial*. Bran pulled one out and handed it to me. "I found those when I was fourteen," he said simply.

"How?"

"I was snooping."

The matter-of-fact confession made me laugh. "What were you looking for?"

"Nothing in particular. I was bored. You were gone for Christmas and I was bringing in your mail. I didn't want to go home. So I started snooping, and I found those."

"I guess I should have hidden them better," I said, although it had never really occurred to me that I might need to.

He laughed. "By the time I was sixteen I couldn't wait for you to go on vacation so I could sneak in here and look at them. I thought about stealing one but I was too afraid of getting caught." Bran was lying on his side, facing me, with his head propped on his hand and his cheeks were starting to turn red again. "I used to come in here just to jack off," he said. "I'd think about you, doing the same thing, looking at the same pictures." His eyes drifted closed, and his voice became lower. "It really turned me on, thinking about you. Thinking about you getting off." Bran opened his eyes again. He reached across to me, putting his hand on my chest, his fingers teasing the hair there. "I know this all seems sudden to you, Will. But I've been thinking about you for a very long time."

"I had no idea."

He smiled. "I have a good poker face." He rolled away from me, sitting up on the edge of the bed. "I should go. I promised to do some work around the house for my ma today, and then she's taking me out for dinner."

"Sure thing." I was surprised at the disappointment I felt at the thought of him leaving.

And as if he was reading my mind, he asked, "Can I see you tonight?"

"Of course," I said.

"It's Saturday," he said hesitantly. "You usually go . . . somewhere." The look he gave me was a question. Of course, he was right. I usually went to the bar on Saturdays.

"I'll be here," I said, and he smiled.

"I can meet you at the pool."

"That sounds perfect," I told him.

I lay there, watching him put his clothes back on. It didn't take long. He'd only been wearing a T-shirt and that treacherous scrap of cloth that roughly resembled shorts. Once he was dressed, he crawled across the bed on his hands and knees and kissed me lightly on the cheek. "Thanks, Will."

"Don't thank me, kid," I said. "It's not exactly altruism on my part."

He smiled at that. "I'll see you tonight."

Since I arrived at the pool ahead of him I started my laps. Not long after, a woman showed up with two kids. She sat in a lawn chair reading while the youngsters splashed and played. When Bran showed up, we said hello and then pointedly ignored each other, floating on opposite ends of the pool. It seemed like they would never leave, but eventually the woman rounded them up, declaring it past their bedtime, and off they went, protesting all the way.

It was completely dark by then, and the weak lights around the perimeter did little to illuminate the pool itself. I was in the deep end, hanging onto the edge so I didn't have to tread water. I could see just enough in the low light to know Bran was swimming very slowly in my direction.

"Tell me you're not having second thoughts," he said.

"No," I told him. "Are you?"

He laughed, a low throaty laugh thick with arousal, and already my body was reacting to him. "Definitely not," Bran said, still slowly moving toward me. He was only a few feet away now.

"We can go upstairs," I said.

He shook his head. "No."

"Surely you don't want to go to your room?" I said.

He laughed. "God, no!" By now, he was in front of me. Bran reached over my shoulder, grabbing the wall behind me to steady himself. "I want to stay here," he said suggestively.

"Here?" I asked uncertainly. My pulse started to race just thinking about it.

"Yes." He pushed closer. His erection ground against my own, and I moaned. He kissed my jaw, and then his tongue touched my ear. "I told you I used to think about you," he whispered, and his free hand slid between us to rub against my erect cock. "This is something I've wanted to do for a long time."

"What if somebody comes?" I asked nervously.

His laugh in my ear was soft and throaty. "That's the idea."

"I meant to the pool!"

He chuckled again and gripped me harder.

Oh God, he turned me on! My ability to protest the locale was fading fast. I felt his fingers pull on the waistband of my swim trunks, and his hand slid inside, scalding me with its heat. His fist found my bare cock and I gasped.

"You can see the gate," he said as he began to stroke. "Just tell me if I need to stop."

In the end I wouldn't have known if anybody walked through the gate anyway. A bomb could have gone off ten feet away and I wasn't sure I would've noticed. He hung onto the wall, and I hung onto him. Bran kissed me hard as I slid my hand into his swimming suit.

And then there was only sensation. The lingering humidity of the hot day, the barely-cool liquid of the pool, his frantic breath against my lips, the sound of lapping water mixed with his quiet moans, the feel of his smooth shaft in my fist, and his strong, calloused hand stroking me, squeezing me, teasing me, until I cried out. He silenced me, his lips sealed hard against mine, and then he came too. I had to grab the wall behind me with one arm to hold us up because he couldn't seem to do it anymore.

When the shaking had passed he pulled away a bit. Even in the low light I could see Bran was smiling.

"That was as fun as I imagined," he said, and I laughed. "I can meet you here again tomorrow night."

"I thought your mom didn't let you swim on the Sabbath."

"I'm not a kid anymore," he said, suddenly serious. "Besides, I think swimming may be the least of my sins."

"Are you worried . . ?"

"No." He moved in and kissed me quickly. "Goodnight, Will."

"Goodnight, Bran."

The next two nights were the same. Bran seemed to love the added anxiety of knowing we were in public with only the dark of night to hide us. It was fun. It had been a very long time since I'd done anything so daring. He made me feel younger than my thirty-five years. But on the third night he asked nervously if we could go to my apartment.

"Of course," I told him, and he followed me quietly up the stairs to my door, and into my room where we both stripped out of our wet suits. He was fully erect, but now that we were in the light again, he looked nervous. "What is it?" I asked him.

He didn't answer. He grabbed me hard, pushing me down onto the bed, grinding against me. "Will," he moaned, sounding frantic and desperate. "I want . . ." his words died in his throat. His eyes held a question he couldn't put into words, hopeful but reluctant to make such a request out loud.

"I know what you want," I told him.

I rolled us over so I was on top, and grabbed the Vaseline from where it still sat on my bedside table. I scooped a generous amount onto my fingers and reached behind me to prepare myself. He watched me with huge eyes.

"You don't have to," he said quietly.

I laughed. "Don't worry, kid. I've done this before, you know." He looked a little bit annoyed, whether at being called a kid or being reminded that this wasn't my first time too, I wasn't sure. I didn't worry about it. I had a feeling he wouldn't be annoyed for long.

I moved myself into position, using my hand to hold him in place against my rim. Anxious anticipation was all over his face and his breathing was ragged. "You won't believe how good this feels," I told him, and before he could answer I slowly sank down onto him, watching his face the entire time. It was an amazing aphrodisiac, seeing the pleasure of it wash over him.

Bran's eyes closed slowly, softly. His breath caught for a moment, and then he moaned, arching his back and pushing deeper into me. "Oh God, Will," he said quietly, and he gripped my thighs hard, his fingers digging into the flesh above my knees.

I lifted myself up, letting him slide almost all the way out before pushing down onto him again. This time his hands moved higher, to my hips. The next time I lifted myself up he pulled me back down, driving his hips up into me at the same time.

"Do you want to be on top?" I asked, and his eyes snapped open in surprise. He considered for a moment, but shook his head. "Do you want to get behind me?" The same second of hesitation, but this time he nodded.

I rolled off of him and onto my hands and knees, and he moved into position behind me. Nothing happened. I was waiting for him to grab me, to push into me . . . Something. But when I glanced back at him, I realized he was still unsure what to do. It was a bit awkward, but I was able to reach behind me and work him into place. I pushed back against him and his head slid into me.

He moaned, finally grabbing my hips and driving himself in deep. And then he froze. "I'm afraid of hurting you." His voice was tight. I couldn't see him, but I could tell his jaw was clenched tight as he fought what he wanted but thought he shouldn't take.

"You won't," I assured him. I reached up so I could brace myself on the headboard. "Go ahead, Bran," I said. "As hard as you want."

There was another second of hesitation, but he finally started to move. He went slow at first. Out and in a couple of times while he found his rhythm. He groaned, a low, hoarse sound. "Oh God, Will," he said. And then, in the blink of an eye, he just let loose, holding hard to my hips and slamming into me again and again. I braced myself with one hand and used the other to stroke my own erection. Our evenings in the pool had been fun and intimate. This was something else entirely—something completely primal—and I was lost to it as much as he was, no thought at all. Only that urgent sense of pain and pleasure, one on top of each other, part of each other, neither one enough to erase the other. I didn't even know which was which, but both of them pushed me further, pushed me higher.

"Bran," I cried out, and then I came hard. As I clenched around him he came too, crying out loud enough I was half-worried the neighbors would hear. I was still shaking when he pulled away and flopped down on his back next to me. There was a sheen of sweat across his brow and he was breathing hard. The smile on his face was enough to light up the whole room.

"Oh my fucking God, that was incredible," he said in awe.

I laughed. "Says the guy who doesn't have to wash the sheets," I joked.

He stretched as he chuckled, sighing happily, and then surprised me by asking, "Can I sleep here tonight?"

"Won't your mom wonder where you are?"

He shrugged. "She might wonder but she won't worry. She thinks I'm seeing someone."

"You are seeing someone," I said lightly.

Bran laughed again. "Right. But I'm not telling her who. Not yet, anyway."

I looked over at him in alarm. "What do you mean, *'not yet'*?"

"I mean, not yet." He shrugged. "I don't want to tell her now. It'll freak her out, and if I don't make it home . . ."

"Don't you say that!"

"I don't want her memory of me to be ruined. But if I do come home . . ."

"What?" I prompted.

"I won't spend my life hiding Will." *Not like you.* He didn't say those last three words, but I heard them anyway.

"What else can you do?"

"Live my life."

I shook my head. "It's not that easy."

"Why not? If I can face a tour in that rotten jungle, then I can face whatever I need to when I get back—"

"People don't like it, Bran. They say it's a sin—"

"I know what they say. But there's places we can go, Will, where it's more accepted. Like in San Francisco, and LA." He was getting excited now, and I could tell he'd been thinking about it a great deal. "That Black Cat Tavern incident really got people talking. And then Stonewall. The Gay Liberation Front has spread beyond New York. There was an article in Time Magazine just last October urging greater tolerance—"

"It also said homosexuality was a *'crippling maladjustment'*," I snapped.

Bran sighed in frustration. "I worked with a black guy on the ranch. He was always talking about a *'race war'*. Well our people are fighting a war too, Will. There are men like us living their lives out in the open. Not hiding at all. Every single one of them is a soldier in our war. When I get home, I'm not hiding anymore either. I'm going to fight."

"Fight who?" I asked in exasperation, but he seemed nonplussed.

"Everyone."

"For what?"

"The truth," he said, as if it was the most obvious thing in the world.

"I think you're nuts."

"Maybe," he said, "but I don't care. When I get home from Vietnam, I'm going to San Francisco. Our people in Cali are going to have one more soldier."

Every morning when I woke, the first sound I heard was his breathing on the other side of the bed, and I would smile. And a heartbeat later would come the realization that it could not last.

"Seven more days," I said to myself when I woke the following Sunday. A knot of dread formed in my stomach.

Bran was on the other side of my bed, still asleep. He looked younger when he was sleeping, and I started to feel a nagging sense of guilt. I angrily pushed it away. He was eighteen. This was what he wanted. In seven days, the US Army would take him away.

I hated the whole fucking world for that.

I reached over with my foot and nudged him. "Bran, it's almost nine."

"Oh shit," he moaned, rolling onto his back and stretching. "I gotta get home."

"I know."

Bran's mom didn't ask too many questions. After the first time he spent the night, he told me she had commented that he had a right to *sow his oats* while he could. Still, he tried to spend time with her during the day. He would, after all, be leaving her too.

In seven days.

He eventually dragged himself out of bed and got dressed. He hesitated in my bedroom door. "I'll see you tonight, right?"

"Of course," I said, and he smiled.

Seven more days.

That night, we went for our usual swim. We played like kids as the sun went down, and once it was dark, he pinned me against the side of the pool, his legs wrapping around mine as he kissed me. I ran my hands down his back, under the waistband of his swim trunks, gripping his firm ass as he ground against me. I always left it up to him whether we finished like this, or in my apartment. Or both.

Tonight, he whispered hoarsely in my ear, "Let's go upstairs."

Once in my room he stripped out of his suit and lay down on his back like he had the first night, with his knees bent and his feet flat on the bed. His skin was tan and his muscles pronounced on his young frame. His erect cock lay on his thick brownish-gold curls, and below it, the root of his shaft seemed to point downward like an arrow, drawing my eye lower between his cheeks, hinting at what I could just barely see below.

"Jesus, Bran," I breathed. "You're incredible."

"What do you mean?" he asked innocently, and all I could do was shake my head.

I crawled onto the bed, between his legs, and he spread them wider for me. Up until tonight it had been only blow jobs and hand jobs, and him fucking me. But tonight I hoped to show him more.

He smelled like chlorine, but his thick, musky scent was there too. It was very familiar by now. I put my tongue on his perineum and licked him from there to the head of his cock. He grabbed my head when I reached the end, trying to push into my mouth, but I pulled away. "Not tonight," I teased.

"I'll do it for you, if you want," he said. He never came right out and said exactly what he meant, but I knew. He was offering to give me a blow job instead.

"Not tonight," I repeated, and the look of confusion on his face was priceless.

I moved back down between his legs, licking and sucking his perineum. I pushed on the back of his thighs, raising his ass toward me just a little. Moving a little lower, I flicked my tongue over that smooth hairless skin, then slid it down, down, to what waited below.

I felt him flinch when my tongue touched his rim. Such an instinctual response when you're not used to being touched there. I smiled. "Relax," I said quietly. "You're going to like this."

I put my tongue on his rim again and very lightly circled it, over and over. Slowly, I felt his muscles relax and heard his breathing start to change. I used my hands to pull his cheeks apart and increased the pressure, pushing against him a little, and he moaned softly. I wasn't sure about other guys, but I knew that for me the edge closest to the front was the most sensitive spot, so I concentrated there, flicking my tongue over it again and again. He relaxed the rest of the way, pushing toward me. I let my tongue penetrate him, just barely, and he gasped in surprise. But he didn't tense up. Bran let his breath out in a rush, and then his legs spread wider. He put his hands under his own knees and pulled them up, giving me much better access.

Such a fast learner.

I pushed my tongue deeper into him and he moaned again.

"Oh God, Will," he breathed, and he pushed toward me, allowing me to reach a little deeper. He let go of one knee to grab his own cock, but I pushed his hand away.

"Hand me the Vaseline," Bran froze, looking scared, and I slapped him playfully on the flank. "Trust me," I said, and he started to breathe again. He handed me the jar, and I went back to licking him, teasing him and pushing my tongue into him until he quit worrying about what I was planning and started to enjoy it again. He was panting hard, pushing toward me, moaning softly. He tried again to grab his own cock, and again I pushed his hand away.

"Will!" he groaned in frustration.

I laughed. "Soon," I told him as I got some Vaseline on my fingers. My saliva might have been enough but I wanted to be sure. The last thing in the world I wanted was to hurt him.

I put my slick finger against his hole, applying just the tiniest bit of pressure. He arched his back, moaning low in his chest. I expected to have to go very slow but it seemed he had other ideas. He reached up to the headboard and pushed, and the entire length of my finger slid into him much sooner than I expected. He moaned again, and his muscles tensed instinctively against the invasion. I waited patiently, stroking his thigh with my free hand. It was only a heartbeat or two and then he relaxed with a sigh.

I began moving slowly, sliding my finger in and out. I flicked my tongue over the head of his cock as I did, never sucking him in all the way, just tasting the salty drops that formed there, teasing him while I let the anticipation build. I moved my tongue down his shaft, over his sac, and sucked one testicle into my mouth. The timbre of his moans deepened as I rolled it gently with my tongue. I moved to the other one, licking and sucking it as I had the first, and still my finger moved slowly in and out of him. I moved back to the head of his cock, flicking my tongue over his slit but refusing to let him push into my mouth. He whimpered a little and I looked up, wanting to see his expression.

"Oh God, Will!" he cried out in desperation, and I knew he was close.

I pulled out of him, and he moaned, this time in frustration. When I pushed back in, I used two fingers, sliding them slowly in as I sucked his cock deep into my mouth. As my lips drifted down his shaft, his hands gripped my head and his fingers knotted in my hair. I felt him start to tense and so I reached that last little bit and pushed against the secret spot inside.

There was no way the neighbors didn't hear him that time. He cried out, a ragged, wrenching cry, part surprise and part relief as he was pushed over the edge, bucking against me, his tight shaft spasming around me as I swallowed again and again, until at last he fell back, panting.

"Holy fucking mother of God, what was *that*?" he gasped.

I had to laugh. His amazement at all things sexual made each act fun for me in a way I hadn't experienced in a very long time. I was starting to think I should seek out virgins more often. "Cool, huh?" I asked.

"'*Cool*' doesn't even begin to describe it," he said.

I moved up and lay next to him and he slid his hand across the bed to rest it lightly on my hip.

"What about you, Will?" he asked.

"I'm good," I told him, and it was true. I'd spent most of my adult life being happy if I could get lucky once a week. We were averaging twice a day. I had absolutely zero complaints.

He sighed happily and stretched, then turned onto his side to look at me. "It's okay if I stay the night, right?"

"Of course." It was surprising how quickly I'd grown accustomed to waking up with him next to me in my bed. I wished we could go on like this forever. I wished I could keep him here, hide him, keep him safe. "Bran," I said, and the words were out of my mouth before I even knew it, "we could go to Canada."

"No."

"We can leave tonight—"

"No."

"I'll go with you if you want, or you can just take my car—"

"No," he said more emphatically this time. "I'm not running away."

I sighed, because it was what I had expected. Bran wasn't the type to hide. "Okay."

"You could come with me to California."

"What would I do there?" I asked, and he laughed.

"Cars break down in San Francisco, too, you know."

I wasn't really sure what to say. I settled for, "We'll see."

We fell asleep side by side.

Six more days.

Bran's mom had taken his last week home off work. He spent his days with her while I worked, but once I got home he belonged to me. It was Friday night, and we had just come from the pool, landing in my bed. I started to move down on him, but he stopped me. "Will," he said hesitantly," I want . . ."

His words trailed away, but it was there in his eyes. The nervous anticipation that I had been waiting for. "I know what you want."

I went slow, holding him and kissing him, using my fingers to prepare him, and finally, pushing gently against him. His eyes clenched shut, and I stopped, not wanting to hurt him. "Bran," I said gently, "look at me." He did. He opened his eyes and met my gaze. "I'll stop if you want," I said, but he shook his head.

"No!" he said

Looking into his gray eyes I saw nothing but unwavering trust. It touched something deep inside of me. "I love you," I said suddenly, surprising even myself. Was it true? I didn't know. I'd never been in love before, and I wasn't sure that was what this was either. But I knew I didn't want him to leave. I knew the thought of him in some jungle on the other side of the world was more than I could bear.

"I love you, too," he said. And then he grabbed the back of my head and pulled me down, kissing me hard. And as he did, he pulled against me, pushing down, and I slid easily all the way into him. We rocked together, our legs intertwined, our breath mingling.

It was the most perfect moment of my life.

Only two more days.

Sunday night was the hardest.

Bran would be leaving the next morning. His mom was driving him to the train station. Part of me wanted to go with them but I knew it would only make it harder. His mother would be there, crying and watching us. We would have to pretend that there was nothing unusual between us. I didn't want our last moments together to be a lie. Instead, he would walk out of my door at seven a.m. and if all went well, I would see him again in eighteen months. If it went wrong . . .

I refused to think about *that* at all.

We made love, and there was no doubt that's what it was this time, even if it hadn't been any other time before. It was slow and desperate and heart wrenching all at the same time. I wanted to tell him again that I loved him, but I couldn't. Feeling him in my arms, his skin slick against mine in the Houston heat, his ragged cries echoing in my ear, I felt like my very soul was dying. I could not stand to let him go.

Afterward, he clung to me as he never had before, and I felt him shaking. I felt the tears on his cheeks. "Will," he whispered, "I'm so scared."

"I know," I said, fighting my own tears. I wanted to be strong for him. "It's okay to be scared," I told him. "But you're going to be fine."

"Promise me you'll come with me," he said. "Promise me that if I make it home—"

"You will!"

"—you'll come with me to San Francisco."

"Let's just get through this, Bran."

"*Promise me!*"

"I promise," I said, not knowing if it was true or not. I wasn't brave like him. I wasn't strong. I wasn't sure if I could do it. But it didn't matter. By the time he got home he wouldn't want me anyway. What mattered now was getting him through this moment. "I promise." He cried in my arms, shaking from the force of his sobs. In that moment the man I loved became again the kid he had once been.

I held him tight, silently mourning them both.

It happened six months into his tour.

We had managed to keep in touch through his training, and even after he'd been deployed I received an occasional letter. But then came the day someone knocked on my door. And when I opened it, his mother. Her face was wet with tears, her eyes full of grief, and my entire world fell into pieces around me.

The funeral was the worst. I hated the guns. Guns had taken him from me. Why did they have to shoot them at his funeral? There were protestors too. They detested the war he'd never wanted to fight, and knew nothing of the one he did. I hated them for thinking they knew anything at all. Bran was better than any of them. *And he was gone.*

I sat at the back through the service, watching his family at the front. I watched them fold the flag and hand it reverently to his mother. *I should be there*, I thought selfishly to myself. *I loved him too.*

Afterward, his mom thanked me for coming. "You were like a brother to him," she said, as if it was a consolation. And again my heart broke inside my chest.

I wanted to shout to the world that I was not a brother, I was not just his friend. I had watched him and helped him and taught him. I had held him and loved him. I had known him as no one else ever had.

Or ever would.

Why should I have to hide it? Why should I have to lie?

Never in my life had I cried the way I did that night. I cursed God, the army, the Viet Cong, and everything else I could think of. None of it did any good. I wished I was brave like him. I wished I was strong. I wished I could make a difference.

Bran would have told me I could. He might have even made me believe it.

I thought about it all night, and when this morning dawned hazy and bright, the Houston heat already seeping into every crack and corner, I had a plan. Bran was right. Cars break down in San Francisco too.

They should have had him. But they'll get me instead. I'm not hiding any more.

Our people in Cali are about to have one more soldier.

Cinder: A CinderFella Story

1

Once upon a time there was a beautiful maiden who fell madly in love with a handsome young knight. They had a magical, whirlwind romance, and then the knight swept his lady off to a far-away land and married her.

But they did *not* live happily ever after.

Ten years to the day after their wedding, they were killed in a fire, leaving me, their only son, behind to be raised by my mother's twin sister. Aunt Cecile was recently widowed with twin daughters of her own. It was bad enough my mother had run off with a knight rather than marrying a proper gentleman, thereby leaving a black mark on the family name, but she had now left me with no money or inheritance of my own. Aunt Cecile already harbored a great deal of resentment. Being saddled with me didn't improve her disposition. And if I sometimes thought fate had been a bit unfair, it was a matter I chose not to dwell on.

The day I met the prince started like any other. I rose early to do chores—stoking the fire, collecting eggs, feeding the animals, and then helping our old cook Deidre prepare a late breakfast for the family. My cousins, Jessalyn and Penelope, were more agitated than normal.

"I'm telling you, mother," Penelope said, "the servants are all talking about it."

Jessalyn glanced pointedly in my direction and rolled her eyes. "Servants?" she said with obvious disdain. "What do they know?"

"Sometimes, quite a bit," Aunt Cecile answered. "Servants hear things. They see things others don't." She turned to me. "Cinder, what have you heard?"

They rarely bothered to talk to me at all, unless it was to give me orders. Cecile's question brought me up short. They'd certainly never asked my opinion on anything. I cleared my throat. "Well, I heard the same things Penelope heard—that the prince is in town. But I also heard there's a group of diamond-hoarding dwarves living in the woods, and that the king from the next country over is burning every spinning wheel in his land because he's afraid of spindles, and that Bella's maid kissed a frog and it turned into a duke." I shrugged. "Servants gossip a lot. I don't believe most of what I hear."

"You see?" Jessalyn said to her sister. They were twins, but not quite identical. Both had long, beautiful dark hair and pleasing faces, but what was pretty on Penelope was ravishing on Jessalyn. Everything about her seemed to shine. Unfortunately, her personality didn't exactly match her lovely exterior. She sneered at me in disgust. "Nothing but lies and rumors."

But Aunt Cecile wasn't ready to dismiss it. "Who says the prince is here?" she asked me.

"Well, I heard it from Tomas who heard it from Anne, who heard it from Tabby. Tabby's maid heard it from her brother. He works at the stable at the inn down the road. *He* told her he talked to one of the prince's guard, and the guard told him—"

"That the prince is coming here to find a bride!" Penelope finished for me. She was practically bouncing in her seat from excitement.

"Right," I concluded. "That's what I heard."

Jessalyn eyed me with cold calculation, then turned to regard her sister and mother. She hated to be seen to agree with me on anything, but she also wasn't stupid. It was obvious she had nothing to gain by continuing to insult me and everything to gain by embracing the drama. She was clearly assessing the situation, trying to decide how to switch sides and make it seem as if she'd been in the right all along.

"Penny has a point," she said at last to her mother. "If the prince came here, he would have had to stay at the inn on his way, and Tabby's brother does work there. And if it's true the prince is coming here to find a bride, then we need to be prepared. You want us to make a good impression, don't you?"

Aunt Cecile smiled indulgently at her daughter. "Of course I do."

And so it was that Aunt Cecile bundled Jessalyn and Penelope into the carriage and headed for the seamstress to secure new dresses for them both.

"It'll take more than pretty dresses to get either of those two ninnies into the palace," Deidre said to me, once they'd gone. "Ugly girls!"

"They're not ugly, though," I said. "Jessalyn especially has a good chance of catching the prince's eye."

"Bah!" she spat. "He can have her. If all he wants is a pretty face, then he deserves to end up with a brat like Jess."

I suspected the prince would indeed be interested in more than a pretty face—specifically, graceful curves and swelling cleavage—but I chose not to share that with Deidre. "I'm going down to the river," I told her. "I'll catch us some fish for dinner."

"Don't forget to leave some for the witch." She told me that every time.

"I won't."

I set off through the woods with my pole over my shoulder. It was a beautiful fall day. Sun shone down through the branches, dappling the mossy ground. Birds sang in the trees. Chipmunks regarded me with suspicion as they scurried across my path. It felt unbelievably fortuitous to be granted a bit of free time on such a gorgeous morning. I whistled as I walked, a barely-remembered tune from my youth.

It felt good to be alive.

Midway to the river was a small clearing in the woods. It was a place I often sat when I had time to spare. Usually, it was empty save for wildlife, but not today. In the middle of the small meadow stood a man. He was about my age, tall and handsome. And he wore only one shoe. I rarely saw anybody in the woods, and it brought me up short.

"Good morning," he said as I stumbled to a halt.

"To you, as well," I managed to reply.

"Lovely day, isn't it?"

"It is."

"Say, watch out for Milton."

"Who?" I asked.

That very next instant, something massive slammed into me from behind, knocking me face first to the ground. An enormous weight on my back held me down. My first thought was that I was being robbed, except I had nothing for them to steal. My second thought was that Milton, whoever he was, had a breathing problem. He was panting heavily into my ear, his breath hot on the back of my neck.

"Milton!" the man scolded. "Let him go!"

The weight disappeared, and Milton, who turned out to be the biggest dog I'd ever seen, rushed panting and wiggling to his master's side. He probably weighed as much as I did. He had short hair and drooping jowls. In his mouth was a shoe.

"Sorry about that," the man said as he took his shoe from the dog. "He's still just a puppy."

"A puppy?" I said, as I got to my feet, brushing dirt and leaves and moss off the front of my shirt. "He's enormous."

"Well, yes. They're bred that way." He turned and threw his shoe toward the woods, and Milton ran gleefully after it. "He's the best hunting dog in the kingdom. Or so they say."

"Who's 'they'?"

"My father's kennel master. They bred him and trained him. They say he could track a phantom stag to the far side of the world. Not that I've ever tested that theory."

"You don't believe them?"

"I believe them. I just don't care."

"Why not?"

"Hunting bores me. I ride along behind Milton while he does all the work, then I have to butcher the animal and haul its stinking corpse back to the palace so they can all gush about it and pretend I did something special." He shrugged. "Plenty of men who hunt because they have to. Let them have the deer. Milton and I prefer playing fetch."

I was hung up on one word. "Palace?" I asked. And then the magnitude of my stupidity caught up with me.

I dropped quickly to my knees, lowering my gaze to the ground. Here I was, facing the prince, and I'd been talking to him as if he were just another servant. "Your Highness, please forgive me. I didn't recognize you."

"Why would you have? We've never met."

"My behavior was inexcusable."

He laughed. "On the contrary. I wear no sign of my title, save my ring, which you could hardly see from all the way over there. We've never met before, which means you had no way of knowing who I was. Therefore, it seems to me your behavior is *entirely* excusable."

I risked raising my eyes. He was looking down at me with obvious exasperation.

He sighed. "For heaven's sake, get up!"

First I felt foolish for not having recognized him, and now he'd made me feel foolish for thinking I should have. I got to my feet again, brushing leaves from my knees. Milton returned the shoe, and the prince turned and threw it again toward the woods. He seemed to have forgotten I was there. I stood watching them play fetch, wondering what in the world I should do next. On one hand, I should not be talking to him, and if I continued to do so, I'd undoubtedly say something foolish. He was, after all, a prince, and I was nothing but a servant in my aunt's house. It was inappropriate for me to speak to him without being spoken to first. On the other hand, I couldn't leave without being excused.

I reached down and retrieved my fishing pole from the ground, where it had landed when Milton knocked me down.

The movement seemed to catch his attention, and he turned to me. "Are you leaving?" he asked.

"Sire, with your permission—"

"Stop!" He sighed as he threw the shoe again for Milton. He shook his head. "I liked you much better when you thought I was nobody special."

That brought me up short. He'd liked me? My heart skipped a beat at the thought.

But now he didn't like me anymore.

"What's your name?" he asked.

"Cinder." Except that wasn't technically correct. Cinder was my surname, and it was what my aunt and cousins called me. Nobody called me by my first name. "Eldon."

He raised his eyebrows at me. "Well, which is it?"

"It's Eldon Cinder."

"It's wonderful to meet you, Eldon," he said. "I'm Augustus Alexandre Kornelius Xavier Redmond." He laughed. "But you know that now, don't you?"

"Yes, Sire."

"Don't call me 'sire.'"

"But—"

"My father calls me August. My mother calls me Alex. You can call me Xavier."

"That wouldn't be appropriate."

"Appropriate is boring." He turned to me again. "Where are you going?"

"Fishing."

"Really?" he asked, suddenly alert and interested. He eyed the fishing rod I held. "With *that*?"

What kind of question was that? I looked at the pole, trying to see what about it was remarkable.

"You really catch fish with a stick?" he asked.

"It's a fishing pole."

"How does it work?"

I might have thought he was trying to play me for a fool, but his expression wasn't mocking. He seemed genuinely intrigued. "Haven't you ever fished before?"

"My father says fish are for peasants. He refuses to let it be served. But once, I sneaked down to the servant quarters, and they gave me some. It was delicious!"

I was trying to decide if I was offended by the peasant comment. He seemed oblivious. He eyed my rod again. "Do you stab them?"

"No! I put bait on the hook, and when a fish swallows the bait, I pull it out of the water."

"So you catch them one at a time?"

"How else would I do it?"

"I have no idea," he said, smiling. "I've never much thought about it." Milton came back again with the shoe, but instead of throwing it, the prince stared at me, his eyes bright and merry. "You're going there now?"

"Yes."

"Perfect," he said, pulling his shoe onto his bare foot. "Lead the way!"

And so I did.

It was strange, walking through the forest as I always did, carrying my fishing pole, but this time with a prince at my heels.

I glanced back to see if he was really there. He was staring up at the treetops, paying no attention at all to where he was going. If I'd done that, I would have tripped and fallen on my face. Apparently princes were granted a bit more natural grace.

Milton barked and frolicked around us, dashing ahead to scout the path, then running back to us as if to say, 'Hurry up, will you? I don't have all day!' Then he'd dart off again, howling and baying as if he was on the trail of some mighty prey.

The forest was silent in our wake. Even the trees seemed to be holding their breath, waiting for Milton and his two plodding humans to pass. I felt as if I should say something, but I had no idea what. How did one start a conversation with a prince?

"Why do you keep looking at me like that?"

I hadn't quite realized I was doing it until he called me on it, but he was right. I'd been staring at him as much as I was able with him following me. I shook my head. "This has to be the strangest thing that's ever happened to me."

"Going fishing?"

"Going fishing with you, yes."

"Are you saying I'm strange?"

I laughed. I couldn't help myself. "Well, you're the prince, and you're following a servant to go fishing. Does that seem normal to you?"

"I suppose not. But you're not exactly normal yourself, are you?"

"What makes you say that?"

"You know who I am, and yet you're not falling all over yourself in an attempt to curry some type of favor from me."

"Would you prefer that?"

"God, no. But that's how it usually works. Everybody wants something. Money, or a job for their father, or a marriage for their daughter." He smiled over at me. "Go ahead. Tell me what you'd ask for."

What would I ask for? I had to think about it. Certainly money or a job outside of my aunt's house might have been nice, but it wasn't the desire that lurked in the deepest recesses of my heart. "Can you bring my parents back?" I asked.

"From where?"

"From death."

The smile faded from his face. "I'm afraid that's a bit beyond my abilities."

He seemed to be taking the request seriously, and I tried to laugh, although it came out flat. "I didn't really think you could."

"Did they die recently?"

I shook my head. "A long time ago. I was just a boy."

"I'm sorry."

We'd veered into something I didn't want to dwell on. It was definitely time to change the subject. I was relieved when

Milton came bounding back, ears flapping and tongue lolling. His innocent doggy joy gave me a reason to laugh. "Are the rumors true?" I asked, as Milton turned and darted back into the woods. "Are you here to find a bride?"

"Is that what they're saying?"

"The town's abuzz."

"Bad news travels fast."

"So it *is* true?"

"I'm the prince, but not the Heir Confirmed. In order to be the true heir to the kingdom, I must be named crown prince."

"And to do that, you have to be married?"

"The law says I must take a bride by my next birthday."

"And when is that?"

"In two weeks."

"Cutting it a bit close, aren't you? What happens if you don't?"

"I'll be forced to renounce my crown, my title, and all claim to my inheritance."

"Ouch."

"No kidding."

"Why here? Seems like a long way to come to find a bride."

He glanced sheepishly my way. "I'd already rejected all the young ladies back home, so my father brought me to your township with the explicit order that I *would* find a wife."

"And here you are, hiding in the forest with your dog."

"I didn't say I intended to cooperate."

"You don't want to be the crown prince?"

He looked down at the forest floor, shoving his hands deep into his pockets. "I want very much to be my father's heir. I just don't want to take a bride."

I wasn't sure what to say to that, so I chose to say nothing at all. We reached the riverbank, and Milton, who bounced around us in glee.

"What about you?" Xavier asked. "Are you married?"

"No."

"Why not?"

Partly because I'd never desired women at all. I found men much more appealing, but I didn't want to tell him that. "I'm just a servant," I said. "Not even that, really. I'm not even paid a proper salary. I'm not exactly the most eligible bachelor around."

"It's funny, isn't it?" Xavier said. I turned to find him watching me, a spark of amusement in his eye as he scratched behind Milton's rather impressive ears.

"What?"

"We have opposite problems. Everybody wants to marry me."

"And that's bad?"

"The thing is, it has nothing to do with *me*, and everything to do with the crown. They don't even know me." He flashed me a mischievous grin. "I could be a lecherous, drunken louse, with base and criminal impulses, and still the fathers would be lined up down the lane, ready to sell their daughters to me like chattel."

"I never thought of it that way."

"I find the whole thing barbaric."

I thought of my cousins, off buying new dresses in hopes of catching the prince's eye. Deidre had been right—it would take more than a pretty face and a silk gown to secure their prize. I couldn't help but laugh. "And *are* you a lecherous, drunken louse?"

His laugh was loud, and he clapped me on the back. "Only on my good days."

His fascination with my fishing pole was short-lived, but he stayed with me as I fished. He sat on a rock, alternately playing fetch with Milton and whittling at a piece of wood he'd found on the ground. He never seemed to stop asking questions, and I found myself telling him about my parents, and Aunt Cecile, and my cousins.

"You told me you were a servant," he said. "But you're her nephew."

"She prefers not to be reminded of the fact." And truth be told, so did I. At one time, I had longed for her to be a mother to me, but those days were long past.

I stayed far longer than I should have. The sun was falling in the sky, and Deidre would be waiting for the fish.

"Must you go?" he asked as I gathered my things.

"I'm afraid so. My Aunt will have it in for me as it is."

"May I walk with you?"

I was struck once again by the absurdity of being asked such a question by the prince, as if he needed my permission. "Of course. I could invite you back to the house for some fish. I'm sure my aunt would be happy to have you—"

"Dinner with the marriageable cousins?" he joked. "I'd rather not. Besides, Milton has terrible table manners."

I laughed, mostly out of relief. I was glad he'd declined the invitation. He would have been at the dining room table with the family, while I served them. He knew my place in their household, but the idea of having him witness it was too painful to bear. My aunt would go to great lengths to humiliate me. Watching Jessalyn and Penelope fawn over him would only make it worse. As it was now, he was a secret—a wonderful, joyous secret belonging only to me. The last thing in the world I wanted to do was share him.

"This isn't the way we came," he said as he followed me through the woods. "I hope you're not following Milton."

Milton had darted ahead of us again, seemingly trying to sniff every tree he saw. "I have a stop to make first."

"Where?"

"There's an old lady who lives here. I leave fish for her."

He didn't say anything else, just followed along behind as I made my way to the witch's cave.

"What kind of person lives in a cave?" he asked, as I lay the fish on the flat stone by the door.

I shrugged. "They say she's a witch. She can do magic."

He waved his hand at me dismissively. "I don't believe in magic." He peered into the mouth of the cave, but there was only darkness. Milton sniffed at the entryway, but seemed unwilling to venture inside.

"They say she can turn pumpkins into carriages and mice into horses."

He frowned at me. "That doesn't seem very useful."

I hadn't really ever thought about it much. What was the point of that kind of magic? "I suppose she could sell the horses."

"Then why don't you leave her mice? And why does she live in a cave?"

"I don't know," I said, trying not to be annoyed. He was a prince, after all, and his questions were valid, even if they did make me feel silly.

"Have you ever seen her?" he asked.

"No."

"How do you know she exists?"

"The fish I leave are always gone."

"You're probably keeping a big bear fat and happy."

I shrugged, feeling foolish. Deidre had taught me to always leave an offering for the witch. It seemed harmless enough, but now I regretted having let him see me do it.

"I've upset you," he said.

"No." Although I wasn't sure if it was true or not.

He watched me thoughtfully for a moment, then pulled something out of his pocket. He placed it on top of the fish. It was a small carving—the one he'd been working on as I fished. It was a dog, rough and inelegant, but clearly modeled on Milton. "Maybe the bear likes knick-knacks, too."

It wasn't really for the witch. It was for me. It was a peace offering, and I accepted it with a smile.

He continued to follow me as we left the witch's cave behind, eventually arriving in the clearing where we'd first met. I turned to face him, feeling awkward. He was tall and regal, and I wondered how I could ever have looked at him and not seen his nobility. Even with Milton panting at his feet, he practically radiated power. "I feel like I should bow or something."

He rolled his eyes. "Please don't."

I couldn't just say goodbye and walk away. That felt entirely wrong. Instead, I extended my hand to him. "It was a very great honor to meet you."

He smiled at me, reaching out to shake my hand. His fingers were strong and warm. "The honor was mine. Thank you for teaching me to fish."

"You're welcome, Sire." His eyebrows lowered, his smile turning into a glare, and I quickly amended, "Xavier."

I wanted to stay longer. I wanted an excuse to touch him again. I wanted this glorious, magical day to go on forever. But I had no way to make time stand still.

Reluctantly, I turned to leave. I was just entering the trees when he called out to me.

"Will you come again tomorrow?"

I turned to face him, although he was halfway across the clearing. "I'm not sure if I can."

"I am the prince, you know," he said. "I could command you to come."

I couldn't tell if he was serious or teasing. "I would have to tell my aunt. Is that what you want?"

"No." His gaze dropped to the ground. "I suppose I hadn't thought of that."

He seemed genuinely disappointed. The thought of it made my mouth dry. It caused a stir of butterflies in my stomach, and a rush of joy inside my chest.

Maybe. If I rose early. If I hurried through my chores. "I'll try to get away after serving lunch," I said.

His gaze met mine, and his smile was bright and gorgeous and unbelievably infectious. "I'll be waiting."

Aunt Cecile had let the other maids go years before, in order to save money. At first, my cousins had railed at the unfairness of being required to dress themselves. It wasn't long before any modesty they'd ever felt in my presence was overcome by a need to have somebody lace their corsets and brush their hair. Somehow over the years, I'd become embarrassingly adept at it.

My cousins knew the prince was in town, and because they seemed to feel there was a chance they might see him at the market (and I dared not tell them otherwise) I was required to spend extra time the next day on their thick, dark tresses. It was two hours past lunch when I finally managed to get away. I made my way through the woods with my heart lodged tight in my throat.

I felt silly. He was a prince, and I was a servant. Did I truly expect to find him waiting for me in the meadow like some heartsick lover? Did I really believe he had no better way to spend his time?

It was with a mixed sense of anticipation and dread that I neared the clearing, my fishing pole clutched firmly in my sweaty hand. I found him there, waiting, just as he'd promised. He was sitting on a fallen log in the middle of the clearing, alternately throwing his shoe for Milton and carving at a piece of wood. Milton nearly knocked me over in his excitement and Xavier smiled broadly at me as he stood, tucking the piece of wood into his pocket.

"You're here!" he said, spreading his arms as if to embrace me.

"Yes, Sire." I tried to sound respectful, as I felt I should, but it was hard with such an enormous grin taking over my face.

He scowled good-naturedly at me. "Don't call me 'sire.'" He eyed my pole. "Fishing again?"

"It gives me a reason to be gone." Otherwise, they'd wonder where I was all day. They'd come up with other chores for me to do.

Xavier retrieved his slightly-squished boot from Milton's mouth. "I suppose I either have to reveal myself to your marriageable cousins or make peace with the fish."

I smiled. "I believe that's correct, Sire."

"The fishes it is, then!" he said, pulling on his boot. He glanced over his shoulder at me as he turned toward the river. "And stop calling me 'sire!'"

And so it was that my friendship with the prince became the center of my life, for a few short days, at least. Each afternoon, I managed to spend a few glorious hours in his presence. He'd meet me in the clearing, and he'd sit with me as I fished. Afterward, I'd leave two fish for the witch, and Xavier would leave whatever he'd carved that day—one day a fox, the next day a kitten, the third day an owl. Then he would follow me to the edge of the clearing and ask, "Will you come again tomorrow?"

Of course I would. I would have moved heaven and earth to see him each and every day. Still, his presence was not without consequence.

My cousins were cranky and sullen. New dresses, powders and perfumes, plus hours of grooming in hopes of catching Xavier's eye, and yet it seemed the prince had barely been seen by anyone, in or out of the palace. He wasn't at the theatre. He wasn't at the shops. He wasn't even in the library, and Jessalyn bemoaned an entire two hours spent checking the aisles, finding nothing but moths and some dusty old books.

Aunt Cecile oversaw the housework with a newfound zeal. "What if the prince comes to call?" she asked at least once a day. "Will you have him find us in squalor?" Some days, it was all I could do not to blurt out that the prince had no intention of ever visiting her home. He'd made it quite clear he intended to stay far away from my "marriageable cousins."

Not surprisingly, my attention to my chores became scattered at best. My sudden distraction did not go unnoticed. Aunt Cecile remarked at dinner that the glasses still had lipstick marks from the day before. Penelope complained her laundry had been washed, but not put away. Jessalyn noted the fireplaces hadn't been swept in days.

All three of them were getting rather tired of eating fish.

I ignored them all. The only thing I cared about was spending as much time with Xavier as I could. I stayed a bit longer with him each day. I knew I was asking for trouble and yet I couldn't seem to help myself. He was somehow invincible—a force of nature I couldn't stand against. A flood that carried me with or without my consent. If he beckoned, I felt compelled to follow. I was light as a feather, and he was the wind.

It wasn't because he was the prince. At least, that wasn't the *only* reason. Certainly having the attention of somebody so important was flattering, but that wasn't why I hurried to the meadow each day to meet him. The real reason was far simpler. It was the fact that he waited for me. He smiled at me. He asked about my day. He listened when I talked. He laughed at my jokes. He asked nothing of me, except for the apparent pleasure of my company. He never commented on my low social standing, or my worn and tattered clothes. He never mentioned the calluses on my fingers, or the ashes in my hair, or the soot that stained my hands. And yet, he listened to me. He met my eyes when I talked. He spoke to me as an equal. He treated me as a friend.

He saw *me*, in a way nobody else in the world did. I was real to him. I mattered.

It was the most amazing gift I'd ever been given.

We had fun together, although we rarely did more than fish and talk while playing fetch with Milton. I looked forward to it every day. Every minute I was not in in his presence I spent thinking of when I'd see him again.

On the fourth day, though, I knew something was wrong. He wasn't his normal, jovial self. He sat on his usual rock next to the river, fidgeting with the ring on his finger, seemingly oblivious to everything around him. Milton had long since given up on fetch. He'd run off into the woods to find his own doggy adventure.

I waited for him to snap out of it, and when he didn't, I spent a long time debating whether I should ask what was bothering him. He was my friend—of course I should ask. But he was also the prince. It was none of my business.

"You seem upset today," I said at last. I tossed my line in the water and turned to watch him closely for signs I'd overstepped my bounds.

He didn't seem bothered by my words. He stared at his hands, fiddling with his signet ring. "My father's quite cross with me, you know."

"Why is that?"

"All this time, he thought I'd been out courting a potential bride."

"And he found out otherwise?"

He continued to twist the ring on his finger. The ring symbolized his status as the prince. To him, it probably underscored the fact that he was not the crown prince. "I have something to tell you." His tone was so somber, somehow foreboding. "My father has taken matters into his own hands."

"He's chosen a bride for you?"

"No." He shook his head, looking up at me at last. "Not yet, at least."

"Then what?"

He smiled, although not his normal, bright smile. He seemed sad. "I'm sure your marriageable cousins will tell you all about it when you get home."

My cousins?

"Will you come to the clearing tomorrow, Eldon?"

"I'll try, of course, but—"

"Can you come earlier in the day?"

That would prove difficult. My aunt and cousins were already cross with me. "I don't know if I can."

"The thing is…." He hesitated, and I was surprised to see a slow blush creeping up his cheeks. "Tomorrow will be the last day I'll have with you."

Was it possible my heart stopped beating? The world seemed to spin around me. I felt sick.

Of course I'd known he wouldn't be around forever, but somehow, I'd let myself forget just how little time I might have with him.

One more day?

It wasn't enough. It would never be enough.

I had to swallow hard against a knot in my throat. I became aware of my fishing pole in my hand, the line being dragged away in the river as I stood there. It felt symbolic. I was as insignificant as my lure, and Xavier was the current. He'd carried me for a while, but I could only go as far as my line allowed. He'd move on—down the hill, around the bend, toward the falling sun—and I'd still be here, on the bank of the river.

Only now, I'd be alone.

"Eldon?"

I had to force myself to speak. "Yes?" My voice came out a whisper. He probably couldn't even hear me over the sound of the rushing water.

"I won't be able to stay late tomorrow, but I'd really like to see you before I go."

"I'll be here."

My cousins were indeed buzzing with news when I arrived home. The king was throwing a ball.

It wasn't like any other ball I'd ever heard of. Every maiden in the township was invited, but none of the men. Each girl was guaranteed one dance with the prince, and his bride would be chosen that evening. After that, the royal family and the princess-to-be would head back to the capital, and I'd never see him again.

I rose early the next day. I rushed about in a frantic effort to finish my chores so I could meet him, if only for a few minutes. But my cousins had other plans.

There was only one seamstress in town, and she'd been barraged by frantic women in need of dresses for the ball. My cousins didn't take priority. They knew they had to make do with what they had. Penelope bore it well, but Jessalyn was in a rage. We rushed about all day, trying to find something she approved of. We raided Aunt Cecile's closet, and called on the married woman next door as well. Deidre did most of the sewing, but it seemed she constantly needed my help. Ruffles and petticoats were removed and re-sewn, necklines lowered, sleeves shortened. I was sent to town three different times, once for a sash, once for gloves, and a third time for earrings in an exact shade of blue. I felt each second tick by. The sand through the hourglass mirrored my hope as it drained away.

I'd never make it in time.

After that, I had to do their hair. Long, loose waves for Penelope, then Jessalyn's up in an artful tangle of curls. I was a bit more forceful than usual as I strapped them into their corsets. Luckily, they were desperate enough to have tiny waists. They didn't object. And finally, they were bundled into our carriage and sent on their way.

At last, I was free.

I rushed through the forest. How long might he have stayed? Would I have a few minutes? The sun was already dipping low behind the tops of the wind-blown trees.

Just let me say goodbye.

I stumbled into the clearing at last, and whatever hope I'd had left died inside my chest.

It was empty.

"Xavier?" I called. Maybe he had only just left. Maybe he'd hear me and come back. But there was no answer.

With a heavy heart, I made my way to the center of the clearing and the fallen log he always sat on as he waited. Sitting on top of it was a gift. It was one of his carvings. The others I'd seen had been rough—recognizable, but done halfheartedly as we talked. This one, though, he'd clearly spent time on. It was a fish. Only a fish, no longer than my little finger, and yet it was beautiful. Its body curved, as if it were leaping from the rapids. Its tail was as delicate as lace. Its tiny scales were perfect.

I cupped it in my hands, and I let my tears fall. There was nobody to see me. There was nobody to know. I sank to the ground, curled against the log, and I cried.

He was my only friend, and he was gone.

I cried as the sun finally sank below the horizon. I cried until I fell asleep.

I woke to the low drone of cicadas. The western edge of the sky was still brushed with pink. The moon was beginning to rise. I hadn't been asleep long.

It took me a moment to take stock. I was in the clearing. Xavier was gone.

Behind me, somebody cleared their throat.

I turned around, hoping to see the prince. Instead, I found a woman sitting on the fallen log. Her body was covered in a gray shroud that was little more than a rag. I'd never seen her, but there was only person she could be: the witch.

"He waited a long time," she said. Her voice was scratchy and harsh, as if she smoked incessantly, although I saw no pipe in her hands. "He paced and fretted, but at last he went away."

She was hard to look at. Or, more specifically, she was hard to see. It was as if my eyes refused to focus on her. One minute, she seemed young as a maid. The next, she was older than Deidre. In the span of a few seconds, she seemed to be anywhere from twenty to ancient. Her hair, too, changed from one moment to the next, sometimes appearing blond and brilliant, at others gray and ratted. It might have been a dream, but the dampness of the ground I sat on and the kink in my neck told me otherwise.

"No fish for me today, boy?"

I cleared my throat and made myself speak. "No."

She laughed. Her voice may have been rough, but her laugh was melodic. Her voice spoke of age, but her laughter of youth. "I was growing weary of it anyway."

I glanced down at the wooden fish in my hand. I stroked its arching back. "I think I'm done fishing for a while." I wasn't sure I could bear to go without Xavier to keep me company.

"And what about that trinket you hold? I'd like to have it. I was looking forward to adding to my collection."

I closed my hand around protectively around the carving. "This one is for me."

"What's it worth to you?"

"It's all I have of him," I said, my voice quiet. "Please don't take it from me."

"What if I could give you something better in exchange?"

"You can't."

"Ah, so little faith." Her tone was chiding, but her eyes were kind. She smiled at me. At the moment, she seemed to be a woman just past the bloom of her youth, still regal and beautiful, but with the wisdom of accumulated years. "Tell me, young Eldon, what would you ask of me?"

Her words reminded me of Xavier and the day we'd met. I remembered so clearly the way he'd smiled at me as he'd said the words. *Go on. Tell me what you'd ask for.*

Back then, I had asked for my parents, but that wasn't the desire that now ruled my heart. "I'd ask to see him one more time."

"Just to see him?" she asked. "Would catching a glimpse of him be enough?"

I shook my head, looking again at the wooden fish tucked into my hand. "To speak to him," I said. "To say goodbye."

"Most people want the world. Most would ask for wealth, or true love. Any girl in the kingdom right now would ask to be his bride."

Of course they would, but I wasn't one of them. I was just a servant who'd gone fishing on the right day and been befriended by a prince. I'd already had more of him than I could ever have hoped.

"I only want to say goodbye."

She was silent. When I glanced up at her, she'd changed again. She was older now, although still not *old*—a middle-aged widow with a touch of gray in her hair and laugh lines around her eyes. "Would you like to go to the ball?"

"Only women are allowed in."

"Minor detail," she said. "Would you like to go?"

I thought about what she was hinting at. Would she sneak me in as a servant or a coachman? "Would I be able to see him? To speak with him?"

"Every maiden is guaranteed a dance."

"Every *maiden*?" The full impact of what she was implying finally hit me. The thought was both exhilarating and terrifying. "You'd make me a woman?"

"Is there any other way?"

Whether there was or not, I didn't know, but I knew I had no desire to be female.

"Don't worry," she said, as if reading my mind. "The spell will only last one night."

One night. One spell. One dance. And in exchange? I thought of the wooden fish clutched tight in my hand.

"Deal."

She held her hand out for the fish. I handed it over, telling myself it would be worth it.

I *hoped* it would be worth it.

"Give me your hands," she said.

I did as instructed. Her fingers on mine were dry and cool. Her hands felt fragile.

"Brace yourself," she said.

"Will it hurt?"

She smiled. "No. But you may find it disconcerting."

And then, she cast her spell.

I wasn't sure what I expected. Magic wands and chanting? Maybe a song and a shower of stars? The witch's spell included none of that. She closed her eyes. She continued to hold my hands. Her lips moved, but no sound emerged. She swayed a bit on her feet.

It started as a warm, tingling sensation in my fingertips and spread quickly up to my wrists. I gaped in surprise at what was left in its wake.

I now had the small, soft hands of a woman.

The warmth continued up my arms. My wrists became thin and delicate. The hair on my forearms seemed to withdraw into my flesh. My skin became smooth and pale.

The magic reached my torso and spread up my neck and down my spine. My shoulders narrowed. There was a tightening in my scalp, as if somebody were gently pulling my hair. My facial structure shifted, my ribcage shrank, my hips widened. The strangest sensation of all came next—the feeling of my center of gravity falling from somewhere above my navel to a spot between my hipbones. It was as if the ground had suddenly risen up to meet me, and yet, I also felt taller. I looked at the witch, who was still swaying with her eyes closed. She was still the same height in relation to me. I hadn't actually grown at all.

Along with the changes to my body came a change to my attire. My worn and tattered clothes were gone. The tightness of a well-laced corset constricted my ribcage, limiting my air. I now wore a flowing, satin gown. It was light green with a long, heavy skirt and a plunging neckline. I blushed as I looked down at the cleavage it revealed.

My cleavage!

I was shaken by a sudden sense of vertigo. I closed my eyes and attempted to take a deep breath to calm myself, but the corset prevented me from getting the oxygen my brain screamed for. The witch's grip on my hands tightened. I opened my eyes. My vision seemed a bit spotty, but I could see her, watching me. She appeared to be older now, her face drawn and wrinkled.

"It's done," she said.

I sat down on the log and took several slow breaths. I couldn't breathe deep, but I forced myself to inhale and exhale until my vision cleared.

"How long will it last?" I asked.

"Until just before dawn."

It was only now just past sunset. I had plenty of time.

I took stock of myself. Now that the magic had finished, this body didn't feel so different from my own. The most notable difference was the tightness of the corset and the itchiness of the lace petticoats underneath my dress. I now had long, chestnut hair. Strands of it tickled my bare shoulders.

"You look like your mother," she said.

"Really?" I barely remembered my mother's face. I wished I had a mirror. I instinctively reached up to touch my face as if that would allow me to see her. My cheek was definitely not my own. It was smooth, with no hint of stubble.

"Don't let your aunt see you. Anybody else will likely mistake you for your cousins, but your aunt will think she's seen a ghost."

Of course. I hadn't thought of that. Aunt Cecile and my mother had been twins. And now her girls were twins, and I apparently resembled them. "What about Jessalyn and Penelope?"

She laughed and shook her head. "Their mother is too far past her youth for them to see your resemblance to her, and they're too caught up in themselves to notice your resemblance to them."

It was strange, knowing I wore my mother's body. Somehow comforting and disturbing, all at the same time. I looked down at my hands. I had long, delicate fingers. I wiggled my toes. There was something strange about my feet. I lifted my skirt a bit to peek down.

My clothes had changed, but not my shoes. I still wore my worn work boots, except now they were two sizes too big.

"Oh," the witch said in surprise. "I forgot the shoes."

I pulled my feet out of my boots and examined them. The shape of my toes was familiar, and yet the daintiness of my bones was not. My heel was narrower, and the gentle curve of my ankle was decidedly not masculine.

I was so busy examining my feet, I didn't see the shoes until she held them out to me. They were like no shoes I'd ever seen. They had two-inch heels, and the rest of them seemed to be made of nothing but thin straps of delicate lace. I was sure as soon as I took a step in them, they'd fall apart. They seemed entirely too small, but when I slid my foot inside of them, I found they fit perfectly.

"Stand up," she said.

I did, although I wobbled. The heels weren't outrageously high, but they were certainly higher than any I'd ever tried to walk in. They seemed determined to sink into the soft ground. It was hard to balance. I had to put my weight on the balls of my feet, which meant thrusting my shoulders back. All in all, it was anything but graceful.

The witch watched me, her lips pursing into a thoughtful frown. The gentle wrinkles around her eyes seemed to deepen.

When I finally had my balance, she said, "Let's see you walk."

The first few steps felt ridiculously clumsy, but after that, I felt I had the hang of it: shoulders back, weight on the balls of my feet, trying to keep my torso rigid and still so as not to lose my balance. I thought I was doing well until I heard her groan.

"What's wrong?" I asked, turning toward her.

"You look like a great lumbering oaf. Is that the best you can do?"

"It's not every day somebody turns me into a woman, you know."

"Plodding, clumsy men," she said in exasperation. "You'll be the laughing stock of the ball."

"It's not my fault!"

She shook her head and sighed. "This will take more magic than I thought."

I thought of the fish Xavier had left for me, now tucked somewhere inside her robes. "I have nothing else to give you."

"I'll fix it," she said. "Leaving you this way would be a waste of a perfectly good spell."

She took my hands, and once again, the magic spread up my arms and over my body. This time, there was no visible change, but there was a definite shift inside my body. I couldn't have said what it was exactly—just a subtle change in my posture, as if I were settling into familiar chair.

"Now let me see you walk."

It was the strangest thing I'd ever experienced. It was like moving though water, except of course there was only air. My brain would tell my body what to do, but somewhere between it and my limbs, something intercepted the message. Something translated the signals into a new language. When I moved, there was a gentle resistance against my limbs which seemed to smooth my movements. There was a new knowledge seated somewhere in my subconscious which told me to put my shoulders back, to arch the small of my back a bit, to let my hips move as I walked in order to accommodate my lower center of gravity.

This time I felt graceful. Even having to adjust for the soft forest floor, I was able to walk the length of the meadow and back without stumbling.

"It's amazing!" I said, feeling excited and giddy. The witch's expression was solemn.

"This spell is more complicated. It won't last as long."

"How long?"

She pulled a watch on a thin silver chain out of her pocket and checked it. "You'll have until midnight."

Midnight.

Suddenly my enchanted evening had been reduced to only a few short hours. What had felt like hope now became something sad and ominous. "That's not much time," I said.

"It's not," she admitted. "I suggest you get going."

The horse cart and rickshaw drivers were out in force, happy to convey anxious young women to the ball in exchange for a few coins. The witch was kind enough to provide me with fare, and in no time at all, I found myself climbing the stairs to the castle.

I was a mess of nervous energy. My palms were embarrassingly sweaty. My heart beat a wild staccato inside my chest as I made my way to the ballroom. What would I say to him when I saw him?

As it turned out, I had plenty of time to ponder the question. A guard ushered me into a room full of women. A steward at the door handed me a small wooden chit with a number on it. "We'll call you when it's your turn," he told me. "After your dance, you can go home, or you can wait in the parlor with the rest."

I eyed the women. Each held a similar chit in her hand. It was disconcertingly like waiting my turn to buy bread at the bakery, except that everyone here was decidedly overdressed. I found an empty seat and settled in.

Some women paced. Some sat quiet and stoic. Some chatted idly with friends. A few were obviously summing up their competition. I spotted my cousins on the opposite side of the room. Penelope sat nervously chewing her cuticles. Jessalyn stood at a mirror, fussing with her hair. Neither of them noticed me.

Jessalyn's number was called next, but she quickly snatched Penelope's chit away and shoved her own into her sister's hand. "You go first," she said. "That way you won't have to sit here worrying any longer."

I knew that wasn't the real reason she wanted Penny to go first. Jess wanted to be able to upstage her sister. Still, Penny didn't argue. She went into the ballroom like a criminal marching to trial. Only a few minutes later, Jessalyn's number was called. I relaxed significantly once they were gone.

More women came in behind me. More left as their numbers were called. The seconds ticked by, and I began to worry I'd have to leave before my turn came. But at last, twenty minutes before the clock was to strike twelve, I found myself walking through the ballroom door.

The ballroom was large, lit with what must have been hundreds of candles. A group of musicians sat in the corner, silent at the moment. Opposite me was another door. My predecessor was just disappearing through it into what must have been the parlor. The prince stood near a buffet table, drinking a glass of champagne. His back was to me.

"X—" I cut myself short, realizing I'd been about to say his name. I corrected quickly and said, "Excellency?" instead.

He didn't turn to face with me. "I'll be with you in a moment."

I approached slowly, moving as quietly as I could in the ridiculous shoes. I didn't want to disturb him, but I didn't want to stand on the other side of the room, either.

As I came nearer to the buffet, I saw it was covered with finger foods and refreshments. They appeared to have barely been touched.

"Not hungry tonight?" I asked.

He sighed and turned to look at me. His eyes were guarded and wary. "My father promised each maiden a dance, not dinner."

It amused me that he would meet his father's demands, and yet go not one step further. "I see."

He gestured over his shoulder at the door the last woman had left through. "There's quite a feast laid out in there, from what I hear, so the ladies don't go hungry as they await my decision."

I pictured another room full of women, much like the one I'd just left. Some would be nervous, some hopeful, some full of resentment. Some would undoubtedly be on their fourth or fifth glass of champagne.

"It sounds wonderful," I said.

He didn't seem to notice the hint of sarcasm in my voice. He looked me up and down with unabashed curiosity. "You look lovely," he said.

"Thank you, Sire. You look…." My words trailed away as I tried to decide how to end my sentence. Every other time I'd seen him, he'd been dressed casually, in clothes that were obviously of the highest quality, and yet designed for daily wear. This evening, he wore something that resembled a uniform. It was royal blue with stiff gold braids on the shoulders and across his chest. Its cut was tight and severe. He was as gorgeous as ever, but he didn't seem at ease.

I still hadn't finished my sentence, and he raised his eyebrows at me. "Charming?" he prompted. "Dashing? Handsome?" He wasn't digging for a compliment. His tone was teasing, and I knew he's probably been told all of those things this evening several times over.

"Uncomfortable," I said.

He laughed. The sound was short, but loud and genuine. "Indeed," he said. "I have renewed sympathy for you women and your corsets."

"You have *no* idea," I muttered under my breath, resisting the urge to tug on the one that bound my ribcage.

"Pardon?"

I decided it was best not to repeat myself. Instead, I gestured to the glass of champagne in his hand. "Do you intend to offer me a drink?"

He smiled. "No, I don't. Do you intend to curtsy like a proper lady?"

Of course I should have done it as soon as he'd turned to face me, but I hadn't thought of it. He was teasing though, not chastising, and I said, "No, I don't."

That made him laugh again. He turned and poured another glass of champagne. He held it out to me. "Happy now?"

I couldn't help but smile. I curtsied as I took the glass, a movement that was somehow unbelievably natural to this body I wore. "Thank you, Sire." My hand trembled as I raised the glass to my lips.

The champagne was unlike anything I'd ever tasted—sweet and bright and bubbly. It was better than anything my aunt ever had in her house. It tasted like morning sunlight. I should have sipped it, but it was too delicious, and I had too little time. I gulped it down all at once, and when I lowered the glass, I found him looking at me with obvious amusement.

"More?" he asked.

I felt myself blush. I didn't often drink. I imagined I could already feel the alcohol flowing through my blood, making me reckless and giddy. I put the empty glass down on the table. "I'm sure a second glass would be unwise."

He held his hand out to me. "Then I suppose this is when I ask you to dance."

Standing there talking to him had been easy, but reaching out to take his hand required every ounce of willpower I had. It felt like something I'd never come back from. His fingers were warm against mine. He pulled me toward him, and as he did, the musicians in the corner began to play.

I'd worried a bit about the dancing, but the witch's spell worked perfectly. I fell easily into step with him. It was strange and magical and amazing. My body moved in a way that was completely unfamiliar to me. It knew which way to step, even if I didn't. I didn't examine this new-found grace too closely for fear focusing on it would ruin the spell.

"You dance beautifully," he said after the first few steps.

"I don't really. It's the magic."

The words were out of my mouth before I had time to think better of them. His eyes widened in surprised amusement. "I don't believe in magic."

"Or course not. I only meant, I'm normally a bit clumsy. It's a miracle I haven't stomped all over your toes, or tripped over my own feet."

"Yes. Well, this is my eighteenth dance of the evening, so I guess we both have good reason to keep the steps simple."

Eighteen dances so far. I thought about the room full of women I'd just left. "There are at least another dozen girls behind me."

He sighed. "I'll be dead on my feet by morning."

"We could ditch the ball and go fishing."

He stopped mid-step, causing me to run into his chest. "You fish?"

I felt myself blush. Why had I said something so stupid? "I shouldn't have said that."

"On the contrary, it's a wonderful idea, except my father would have me drawn and quartered."

"An execution would put a real damper on the evening."

He laughed. "It would indeed."

He put his arm around me again, and we resumed dancing. It was wonderful, being so close to him, letting him guide me in slow circles around the dance floor. He was a force of nature, carrying me somewhere. I didn't know where I'd end up, and I didn't care.

He stared at me as we danced, as if studying me. It might have made me nervous, but I was too happy to mind much. His obvious scrutiny gave me an excuse to look back. I wanted to memorize every angle of his face, so I'd never forget.

"Have we met before?" he asked.

"No."

"You seem very familiar."

"You must be thinking of somebody else—"

"I don't think so. It's something about your eyes."

My heart jumped at his words, partly from joy, partly from an irrational fear he'd guess my true identity. "You must be confusing me with one of the women you danced with earlier."

"I suppose," he said, although it was clear he wasn't convinced.

"So many women, so little light. I'm sure we all begin to look the same."

"Some more than others." He lowered his voice and whispered, as if he were sharing a great secret, "Some manage to stand out."

His words pleased me, and I found myself smiling. "I'm glad I can liven up your dull evening. It must be so hard, spending the hours surrounded by beautiful, fawning women."

He laughed. "Now you're just being cruel."

"And you're being a tease."

He shook his head. There was amusement in his eyes, but something else, too. "You puzzle me," he said.

"Why is that?"

"You're not like any of the other girls."

His words alarmed me a bit. I obviously wasn't playing my part well. "What do you mean?"

"They've all fallen into one of three categories. One: they spend the entire dance telling me how handsome and charming I am. Two: they find me terrifying, and can't even meet my eyes, let alone talk to me. Three: they spend every second of our time together telling me what a wonderful wife they'd be."

"Well, I think you're too charming and handsome to be terrifying, but I'm quite sure I'd make a terrible wife."

"Why do you say that?"

The question made me laugh out loud. If only he knew the truth. "There are too many reasons to list."

He shook his head again. "Definitely not like the other girls."

"I'll try to be more like them, if it will please you. Which of those three options would you prefer? I think I can pull off either of the first two, but the third might be beyond my abilities."

"No," he said. We'd been teasing, but suddenly he seemed serious. "I very much prefer you this way."

I felt myself blush. I could no longer look him in the eye. I found myself studying the gold braid at his throat. I had no idea what to say.

"If you're so opposed to marriage, why are you here?" he asked. "Did your father make you come?"

"No. I...." I stumbled, unsure what to say. He was watching me expectantly. I decided to tell him the truth. "I just wanted to see you one last time."

The song ended, but he didn't let me go. He had that same studious expression on his face, as if he was trying to figure me out. I held very still, wondering what exactly he was thinking. The moment seemed to last forever.

"Will you dance with me again?"

Nothing in the world could have made me happier. "Of course."

He smiled. He nodded at the musicians in the corner. A new song started. And we danced.

It was both nerve-racking and intoxicating being so close to him. Breasts—*my* breasts—were pressed tight between us. I found the feeling incredibly disconcerting, but everything else was perfect: the way he looked at me. The firmness of his hand on the small of my back. He stirred something in me—a dull, pulsing ache between my legs, so different from the feeling of arousal in my own body, and yet, unmistakably recognizable. It made my knees weak. My stomach was queasy, full of butterflies. Every piece of me strained toward him, longing for him in a way I'd never fully realized before. I felt feverish. My body—my *female* body—felt like it was burning up from the inside out. Surely he must sense it. Surely he must recognize the affect he was having on me.

He pulled me tighter against him, and I felt the stiffness of his member against me. It made me breathless. He tilted his head down to me, his lips a centimeter from my own.

"Would it be completely inappropriate if I kissed you?"

My heart soared. I put my arms around his neck and whispered back, "Appropriate is boring."

His mouth was warm and soft. His tongue teased against my lips, and I heard myself whimper. I opened up to him, letting him taste me, letting him explore me. He moaned, a low sound from deep in his throat that caused the heat between my legs to grow. The ache seemed to spread simultaneously down my thighs and up through my abdomen to the breasts that were jammed uncomfortably between us. The room ceased to exist. The music too. Whether the musicians stopped, whether they whispered, or whether they played on, I didn't know and didn't care. I hung onto him, wondering how something as simple as a kiss could feel so unbelievably good.

He broke the kiss, still holding me close. He was as breathless as I was.

"That was amazing," he gasped.

I could only cling to him and nod.

"Why do you seem so familiar?"

I shook my head, not wanting to let him think about it. Not wanting to think about how I should answer. I pulled his head down so I could kiss him again, but he stopped just before his lips met mine.

"What's your name?"

My name. What *was* my name? All that time I'd spent waiting my turn to dance with him, and it hadn't once occurred to me he might ask me such a simple question. I had no idea what to say. I couldn't think of anything except my *real* name. I couldn't give him that.

"Umm…." I said stupidly.

But I was saved from answering by a sound—a terrible, heartbreaking sound.

The sound of the bells in the clock tower striking midnight.

I fled. I ran from the ballroom, Xavier calling after me, first asking and then ordering me to wait.

I had no choice but to disobey.

Faces with wide eyes and gaping mouths turned as I sped past. I was vaguely aware of making such a ridiculous spectacle of myself, but it would be far worse if they saw me without the magic.

Somewhere on the stairs, the first of the spells gave way. One moment I was running in the ornate slippers, and the next I was tripping. The tall heels of the shoes threw my balance too far forward. My ankles wobbled. The movement of my hips became my own. "Plodding, clumsy men," the witch had said, and in the space of a few seconds, I'd become one again, albeit still hidden within the body of a woman. I fell halfway down the stairs, tearing my dress in the process.

How in the world did women manage?

Behind me, I could hear voices calling. Somebody was coming after me. I pulled the ridiculous sandals from my feet and ran. I ducked behind the row of waiting carriages. I was vaguely aware of coachmen and drivers, their eyes wide with shock, as I bolted past them.

"Guess that one's dance didn't end well," one of them laughed.

I ran all the way home, gasping for air against the constraints of the corset I wore, wishing I could tear the damn thing off, but the coachmen might do more than stare if the woman flying past them was bare-breasted.

Finally, I stumbled through our gate, but I stopped short on the walk. The light was on in the parlor. Aunt Cecile was waiting up, anxious for word from her daughters.

I couldn't let her see me—the specter of her dead sister, dress torn, feet bare and caked with mud. I could go in the back door, but even that seemed risky. What if she called to me to bring her tea or stoke the fire?

With a moan, I turned and headed for the only place I could think of. The only place that was mine: the clearing in the woods. The place I'd first met Xavier. The place where I'd met the witch.

The meadow was empty, of course. I fell to the ground in a graceless heap, glad to finally be able to sit. My side ached from running. My feet hurt. I'd lost a shoe somewhere along the way. I felt a bit bad about it. I hoped the witch wouldn't be mad.

It took a few minutes to catch my breath. The crickets had stopped their songs as I passed, but now they began again. Something skittered away unseen in the woods. It was quiet and peaceful. Moonlight shone through the trees, dappling the forest floor.

I wanted to undo the dress and loosen the corset, but the buttons were too high up my back for me to reach. After a minute of stretching and straining, I gave up. One more reason I was glad to not be a woman.

I leaned back against the fallen log Xavier had left his gift on. I'd traded that gift away for two spells, and a few short hours, but it had been worth it.

I thought about Xavier. I relived the dance. I remembered the feeling of him holding me close. The taste of him. The hardness of his erection against me. Heat kindled again in my groin, so familiar, and yet so strange. I remembered the soaring joy in my heart when he'd asked if he could kiss me.

I curled up on the soft leaves of the forest floor. And I thought again, as I drifted off to sleep, *It was worth it.*

I slept fitfully at first, but at some point, the constriction around my chest ceased, the itchiness of the lace went away, and I fell into a comfortable slumber, at home in my own body.

I woke well after dawn. I was myself again, wearing my usual patched clothes. My feet were bare. My worn boots lay on the ground next to me.

On any other morning, I would have been up at dawn. I wondered if Aunt Cecile and my cousins were searching for me. Would they wonder where I'd gone? Would they care? I could only hope that after the late night, they'd all slept in.

I stopped by the well behind the house to clean myself off. My feet were scratched and dirty from my barefoot sprint home. I washed away the dried mud and pulled my boots on before heading inside.

I knew right away something was amiss. I could hear Jessalyn and Penelope in the living room, talking frantically over each other. Deidre turned to glare at me.

"Fine morning for you to be off missing," she said. "They're in a right uproar."

"Over what?"

She waved her hand at me dismissively as she turned back to her stove. "Something about the prince and the ball."

I had work to do. I had no reason to get involved. No reason at all.

Except she'd mentioned the prince. Whatever had my cousins in a 'right uproar,' it involved Xavier. Just the thought of him made my heart skip a beat. I knew I'd get nothing done until I discovered what was going on.

Penelope and Aunt Cecile rushed busily around the living room, dusting and straightening. It was something they usually left for Deidre and me to do. Jessalyn sat in her favorite chair, glaring at them as they worked.

"I don't know why you're bothering," she said. "We know he won't come here."

"We know no such thing," Aunt Cecile said. "They say he picked a bride, and he'll call on her today."

He'd picked a bride?

A sad knot of jealousy clenched inside my chest. Of course he'd picked a bride. That had been the entire purpose of the ball. Still, after the way he'd held me, and the kiss....

"Who is she?" I asked.

They all turned to me. They hadn't noticed me enter, and now they all stared at me as if I'd asked them who hung the moon.

"Nobody knows," Penelope said at last.

"She ran away," Jessalyn said.

"They say the prince was calling after her, but she didn't stop, and—"

"Yes," Jessalyn said, cutting her off. "And that's how we know it won't be one of us. We weren't fools enough to run away!"

My heart skipped a beat. Yes, I'd run away, because I'd had no other choice. Was there any possibility another girl had fled as well? Could he be searching for somebody other than me?

It seemed unlikely.

I didn't know whether to laugh or cry. "But he knows who she is?" I asked.

"They say he doesn't know her name, but he has a way to find her," Penelope said. "Everybody's talking about it."

A way to find her.

A way to find *me*?

I couldn't help myself. I burst out laughing.

Of course he was wrong. He couldn't find her, because she didn't exist. The woman he sought had disappeared in the night, nothing more than a spell. He could hunt, but he'd never catch his prey.

They were all staring at me in shock, and I realized I was still laughing. More than laughing. I was bordering on hysterical, holding my stomach, trying to use the laughter to keep my tears at bay.

He wanted to marry me.

"Cinder, *what* is so funny?" Aunt Cecile asked.

"Nothing," I said, gasping for air, trying to regain my composure. It was true. There was nothing funny about what was happening. "I'm sorry." Not that my apology helped. Aunt Cecile looked disgusted. My cousins, confused. "How will he find her?" I asked.

But before they could reply, I received my answer: the familiar baying of a dog. Everybody turned toward the front window. Penelope rushed over to peek through the curtains.

I didn't need to look. I knew what she would see.

Milton.

"Oh no," I moaned.

They all turned to me in surprise, but before they could ask what was wrong, there was a great, loud knock at the door.

Penelope's pale hand fluttered to her mouth, her eyes wide with excitement and fear. Aunt Cecile was practically bouncing in her shoes. Jessalyn rushed to the door and pulled it open.

A massive, hairy shape raced through the opening, barking and drooling. Milton flew at me, knocking me over backward on to the floor. His paws landed on my abdomen. His weight drove the air from my lungs as I hit the ground. His massive, quivering jaws loomed over my face.

"Milton, you hairy oaf!" a voice I recognized as Xavier's cried. "What's come over you?"

Milton moved off of my chest, and then the prince was looming over me, his face lit by his handsome smile.

"Eldon!" he cried happily. He took my hand and helped me to my feet. "I didn't expect to find you here."

Milton had knocked the wind out of me. I was too busy trying to breathe to answer. My stomach was cramped, my brain screaming for oxygen and apparently not comprehending that it needed only to inhale. I was vaguely aware of the room around me—my aunt and cousins, Deidre, who had come in from the kitchen, the two men who'd entered with Xavier. All of them wore shocked expressions, clearly wondering at the prince's familiar attitude toward a servant.

What wasn't vague at all was the gentle firmness of his hand on my back, so similar to the night before.

"Eldon," he said, "are you all right?"

I finally managed to take a short breath. And then a second. "I'm fine," I gasped, although I still couldn't quite stand up straight.

"I can't think why he bowled you over like that," he said. "He's always liked you, but still." He looked over at Milton, who sat by the fireplace, panting happily. His wagging tail thumped against the wooden floor. The steady *thump, thump, thump* seemed unusually loud in the otherwise quiet room. My aunt and cousins gaped at me, obviously baffled and wondering how Xavier knew my name.

I made myself stand tall, although my stomach still hurt. I turned to him and said, "Sire?" He lowered his eyebrows, glaring at me, and I knew he wanted to tell me not to call him that. I rushed on, before he could. "Perhaps you should tell us why you've honored us with a visit today?"

His eyes swept quickly over my aunt and my cousins, and Deidre, dismissing them each in turn. He glanced hopefully around the room, as if he may have missed somebody, then turned toward the stairs.

"I'm looking for somebody," he said. "Is there anybody else here? Upstairs, maybe?"

"No," I said. Of course I knew who he hoped to find, but it seemed he was waiting for me to say more, so I asked, "Who were you expecting?"

He smiled at me. "A girl." He reached into his coat and pulled something from his pocket. He held it up for me to see.

It was my lost shoe.

"I gave it to Milton," he said, "and Milton led me here."

He turned again to eye my cousins with unabashed curiosity, trying to determine if one of them was the girl he sought. He was confused, I could tell. I had resembled them both and yet, he seemed to not recognize them at all.

"Perhaps Milton was confused," I said.

Xavier shook his head in response. "Impossible. You know he's the best tracker in the kingdom."

Yes. So good he'd managed to track me through a magical sex-change.

Xavier held the shoe up for my cousins to see. In the bright light of day, it looked sad. Wilted. The ornate lace straps seemed wretched. "Does this belong to either of you?"

The room was deathly silent, still as a tomb. Everybody's attention was on the shoe.

Penelope spoke first. "No, sire," she started to say. "It's not ours—"

Jessalyn cut her off. She stepped forward. Her twin sister was confused. Her mother, elated. I felt my heart sink in my chest.

She wouldn't be so low, would she? She wouldn't lie!

But I knew I was being a fool.

Of course she would.

She smiled at the prince and said, "Yes, Highness. It's mine."

Nobody moved. Xavier still held the shoe aloft as studied Jessalyn.

Something stirred in my chest—an angry rebellion. A hurt and jealous beast. How dare she?

"It's not your shoe," I said.

Xavier turned to me in surprise. Jessalyn's dark eyes fixed on me as well, demanding my silence.

"Of course it is."

Xavier glanced back and forth between us, obviously unsure how to proceed. "Perhaps," he said to Jessalyn, "if you could produce the other one?"

She blinked at him, smiling, and whether she really was confused by his question or whether it was an act, I didn't know. "The other one?" she asked.

"Yes," he said with seemingly infinite patience. "The other shoe. They usually come in pairs."

Her face flushed. Her eyes darted from side to side. Could he see the cold calculation in them?

"I lost them both, Sire," she said. "I was in such a hurry to get away, I couldn't run properly."

"Why exactly did you run?"

"Well…." She played nervously with the necklace she wore. She bit her lip. I'd never realized what a wonderful actress she was. "I was so nervous, Your Highness. Being in your presence…I'm afraid I was a bit overwhelmed."

Xavier's puzzlement grew. "Overwhelmed?" he said, as if contemplating the meaning of the word. I knew he was thinking about our dance. Thinking about the fact that, unlike so many of the other girls, I *hadn't* been overwhelmed by him. We'd talked of fishing. And magic.

And we'd kissed.

Jessalyn must have seen his hesitation. She must have sensed his uncertainty. She took another step toward him and said, "I'll prove it, Sire. Let me try on the shoe."

His face lit with a smile. "Wonderful idea!"

Jessalyn sat on the ottoman nearest the prince. She reached down and removed the boot she wore. She looked up at him expectantly.

Xavier held the slipper toward her.

Jessalyn crossed her legs, right over left, holding her bare foot toward him. She tugged her dress a bit, causing the lace-trimmed hem to slide alluringly upward, revealing her pale ankle.

Xavier's face flushed. It was clear she expected him to get on his knee in front of her and help her into the shoe. It was equally clear he had no intention of doing so. He held it out to Penelope.

"Assist her," he said. There was a note in his voice I'd never heard before—a tone of command. A tone he'd never used with me.

Jessalyn hid her disappointment well. Only years of living with her allowed me to see the quick blink of her eye that hinted at her dissatisfaction.

Penelope took the sandal from the prince and knelt at her sister's feet. She held it out. I could barely breathe. The air felt heavy with anticipation.

Jessalyn slid her foot neatly inside.

Something inside of me withered and died. Some dream I'd had. Some secret I'd buried so deep, even I hadn't quite known it was there. Jessalyn's pretty little foot in that stupid lace slipper was like a knife in my chest.

I wanted to throw myself at his feet. I wanted to tell him the truth.

I wanted desperately to be her.

Jessalyn beamed up at the prince. Xavier still seemed uncertain, but he smiled back. "I suppose this is the part where I ask for your hand in marriage."

She jumped up and threw her arms around his neck. He hesitated, but only for a second. He put his arms around her. He buried his nose in her thick, chestnut hair.

He looked happy.

I closed my eyes. I forced myself to breathe. I willed my heart to stop aching. So Jessalyn would have the man I loved as her own. What did it matter? It wasn't as if he could choose me anyway, even if he wanted to.

They were all talking at once. The room was so loud. Plans were already being made. Time was short. The prince had to take a wife by midnight, nine days hence. Jessalyn and Xavier would be leaving the very next morning, heading back to his home to plan the wedding. She'd see him every day. Every day for the rest of her life.

And me? I'd see him when they came to visit. *If* they came to visit.

"Eldon?"

It was Xavier's voice, and everybody else in the room stopped speaking. I could almost feel the weight of their stares as they turned to look at me.

I took a deep breath. I made myself open my eyes and face him. He was smiling. He put his hand on my shoulder. "You'll come, won't you?"

"Sire?"

He scowled at me. I knew he wanted to tell me to call him by his name, but after glancing quickly at Jessalyn, Penelope, and Aunt Cecile, he seemed to think better of it. They were all watching us, obviously listening to our conversation. He stepped closer to me, making me feel that what we shared was special. His hand on my shoulder felt warm and heavy. "It's a fortuitous day. Not only do I find my bride, I gain a brother, too." His voice was low, but it was so quiet in the room, everybody heard him. "It pleases me to have a reason to keep you near."

I ducked my head to hide my smile.

Maybe my heart wasn't so broken after all.

2

The king left for home that very day, as soon as he was assured of Xavier's impending marriage, and I spent the next twenty-four hours rushing around like a fool, trying to get Jessalyn and myself both ready to leave. Xavier offered to take Penelope and Aunt Cecile along too, but Jessalyn protested, saying she didn't want to trouble anyone. Her mother and sister were understandably furious. They were gracious enough not to say anything in front of the prince, but once he was gone, the accusations and arguments began. I was glad. They were all so busy snarking at each other, nobody thought to question me about my friendship with Xavier.

Jessalyn may have claimed she was leaving her family behind out of some misplaced sense of martyrdom, but I knew the truth: she didn't want anybody around who might embarrass her or remind others of her less-than-royal roots. She would certainly have left me behind as well, if she'd had the choice, but Xavier made it quite clear he wanted me along.

And so it was that I found myself on the way to the palace the very next morning, in the company of Xavier, Jessalyn, and a dozen guards and attendants.

And of course, Milton.

Jessalyn rode in a carriage with the prince. He'd started out on horseback like the rest of us, but she'd batted her eyes at him and made some simpering comment about getting to know one another better and he'd relented and joined her, tucked away inside the vehicle, out of sight, out of my reach.

I couldn't hear their conversation, but every so often, I'd hear Jessalyn laugh. I tried to tell myself the jealousy I felt each time was foolish. I told myself my growing hatred of her was unjustified. I wondered over and over again if I should tell the prince that Jessalyn was not who he thought.

We stopped at midday to eat. I helped two of the servants lay out a cold lunch of cheese, ham, biscuits, and fresh strawberries for Xavier and Jess while the other men tended to the horses and ate their own lunches of hard bread and dried meat. Milton eyed the picnic with an attentiveness that was downright alarming. Strings of drool hung from his heavy jowls. I was afraid if we turned away for even a second, he'd swallow the entire spread in one bite.

"Am I really supposed to sit on the ground?" Jessalyn asked. "I'd hate to ruin my gown."

Xavier regarded her with what seemed a mix of amusement and annoyance as she dispatched me to the carriage for cushions and a blanket in order to keep her dress clean.

I avoided his eyes as I helped her get settled across from him. I hated for him to see me as what I was—a mere servant to his bride-to-be. I was afraid I would look at him and see pity in his eyes.

"That's good enough," Jess said, making a shooing motion at me with her hands. "You can go."

I turned to leave, but I was stopped by a question from Xavier. "Why don't you join us, Eldon?" I turned to find him gesturing for me to sit next to him on the ground.

The question caught me by surprise. So did the expression on his face. There was no pity or disgust, as I'd expected. Only the same friendly regard I'd seen on his face every other time we'd been together. Whatever resentment I'd felt for my cousin was wiped from my mind by the warmth of his smile and the sincerity of the invitation.

"Oh Xavier," Jessalyn said, and I wondered if I actually saw a wince of annoyance on his face when she said his name. "A servant lunching with the prince? That really wouldn't be appropriate."

He smiled over at her. "Appropriate is boring."

The statement made me laugh out loud, but Jessalyn only blinked at him in surprise. "On the contrary, I think it's important for us to maintain a sense of propriety when there are servants around."

The smile slowly faded from Xavier's face to be replaced by puzzlement. I knew he was thinking about our kiss, wondering if this woman he was talking to could possibly have forgotten having said those very words to him.

As much as I longed for time with the prince, I didn't want Jessalyn watching us and listening in. I wanted to keep my friendship with him to myself. I wanted to keep it out of the reach of her grasping fingers.

"Thank you for the invitation," I said, "but perhaps I should take care of Milton."

He was disappointed, I could tell, but Jessalyn said immediately, "Good idea, Cinder. Tie him up behind the carriage."

I did take Milton behind the carriage, but I didn't tie him up. Instead, I took off my boot, and the two of us played fetch until it was time to leave.

Xavier chose not to return to the carriage. Instead, he had his horse brought to him. "I'm going to ride ahead and make sure everything's ready at the inn," he said, motioning two of his guards to accompany him. Then he turned to me. "Eldon, will you join me?"

"I'd love to."

"Of course he'd love to, Xavier," Jessalyn said, "but it will have to be another day."

This time, I was sure I saw a flash of annoyance in Xavier's eyes, although it was gone by the time he turned to her. "And why is that?"

She seemed to sense his impatience. She immediately turned on the 'poor me' routine, ducking her head and glancing up at him through her long lashes. She gestured to the rest of the guard. "I don't know any of these men," she said. "You wouldn't leave me in the company of strangers, would you?"

"Do you suspect any of them would be fool enough to harm you?"

"Of course not," she said. "It's just that I'd feel so much more comfortable if Cinder were here with me."

I clenched my hands tight on the reins of my horse. I ducked my head so they couldn't see my expression. I hated to be caught between them, not because I didn't know which direction I preferred, but because I knew the more Xavier pushed, the more miserable Jess would endeavor to make me.

The prince sighed. "Fine," he relented. "I'll see you in a few hours."

He turned without another word and left us, Milton running ahead with a triumphant howl, the two guards following behind.

I was left alone with Jess and ten men I did not know.

With the prince gone, Jessalyn dropped her act in an instant. She turned to me with fury in her eyes. "Get in the carriage, Cinder," she said. "It's time you and I had a talk."

The carriage was awful. Jessalyn had the curtains closed on the one small window, making it dark and stuffy inside. I sat across from her. The space was way too small. I could feel the anger and resentment coming off of her, filling the carriage, making it hard to breathe. I wished I could scoot back and put more distance between us. I thought of how uncomfortable the ride must have been for Xavier, who was several inches taller than me. No wonder he'd decided to ride his horse for the second half of the day.

Jessalyn waited until we were well underway before she spoke. I knew she hoped the sound of the wheels and the road and the horses would prevent the guardsmen from overhearing.

"How do you know the prince?" she asked, her voice pitched low.

"I met him in the forest."

Disbelief flashed in her eyes. "Doing what?"

I didn't know if she meant him or me, so I answered both possibilities. "I was going to the river to fish, and he was playing fetch with Milton."

"And then what? He just decided to talk to you?"

"He asked if he could go fishing with me."

"A *prince* asked a *servant* if he could go fishing?"

"Yes."

"Why? What lies did you tell him?"

"I only told him the truth."

She slapped me. In all the years I'd been part of my aunt's household, she'd never struck me, and it took me completely by surprise.

"Don't lie to me!"

I put my hand to my cheek, as if I could hold the sting of her wrath there. I savored her anger and her jealousy. I had no desire to appease her. "You know all about lying, don't you?"

She went very still. The only movement was the flaring of her nostrils.

"Shall we talk about the shoe?" I asked. "We both know it doesn't belong to you."

"Are you threatening me?"

Was I? Even I wasn't sure. But she didn't give me a chance to answer.

"Think about this, *Eldon*." She'd never called me that before, and I knew she only did it now to remind me of the prince's familiarity with me. "If you tell him, and he believes you, what happens then? Have you thought about that?"

"He'll pick a new bride."

"Yes. And I'll be sent home. And where do you think you'll be?" She smiled at me—a cruel, malicious smile that made my blood run cold—and she gave me the answer. "You'll still be working for me. And I promise you, Cinder, I will spend the rest of my life making yours a living hell."

It was true. It made me sick to my stomach to admit it, but she was right. Unless....

"He might not send me away."

She laughed, and if I'd thought her smile was cruel, her laughter was worse. "When he learns you've allowed this to go on as long as it has, do you think you'll still have his favor?"

It was a good question. Would I? Or would he blame me for not telling him sooner?

"Do you honestly think you can fool him forever?" I asked.

"I don't need to fool him forever. We'll be married in eight days. After that, it'll be too late." She leaned back in her seat. She crossed her arms. She looked smug. She thought she'd won.

Of course, she had. I hated it, but she had a point. I hung my head in defeat.

She knocked on the side of the carriage, and it slowed to a stop.

"Get out of my carriage, *Cinder*," she said. "And if you know what's good for you, you'll keep your secrets to yourself."

The rest of the afternoon was miserable. It was blistering hot. We were plagued by flies. By the time we reached the inn, I was sweaty, stinky, and sunburned. Even the scene with Jessalyn paled when I thought about the bliss of a home-cooked meal and a night in a soft bed.

If it was hot outside, I could only imagine how stifling it had been inside the carriage. I was happy to see that even Jessalyn couldn't emerge unscathed. Her dress was damp and wrinkled. She was sullen and cranky. And she smelled no better than I.

Xavier greeted us at the door. He'd had dinner laid out in a private room near the back.

"I brought champagne," he said, pouring not two, but three glasses. "It's perfectly chilled." He held a glass out to her. "It will refresh you."

"Thank you, my Prince," Jessalyn said as she reached for the glass.

Xavier teasingly pulled it out of her reach. "Do you intend to curtsy like a proper lady?" he asked.

Jessalyn actually blushed up to her sweaty hairline. "My apologies, Highness," she said, as she bent her knee. "Please forgive my oversight."

The surprise on Xavier's face might have made me laugh any other time, but this time, it only served to remind me that keeping Jessalyn's secret was in my own best interest.

"I think the prince was joking, my lady," I said.

"Of course," Xavier said, taking her hand and bringing her to her feet. "But I shouldn't have. After such a long day, it was in terrible taste."

She smiled sweetly at him as she took the champagne. "Thank you." He watched her expectantly as she took a small sip. She seemed to realize he was anticipating some kind of reaction from her, but she obviously didn't know what. She smiled uncertainly at him. "It's interesting," she said. "I've never tasted anything like it."

He was clearly disappointed, but he didn't say anything. He took the second glass from the table and offered it to me. "Have some, Eldon," he said. "I'm sure you could use a drink, as well."

I took a sip, and I discovered why he'd watched Jessalyn's reaction so attentively. It was the same champagne he'd served to me at the ball. I was immediately transported back to that night by the bright, bubbly sensation of sunlight on my tongue, and I did as I'd done then—I tilted my head back and drank it all at once.

"It's delicious!" I said as I handed him my empty glass.

He laughed. "I'm glad somebody appreciates it." I didn't miss the scowl this elicited from my cousin, but the prince didn't seem to notice. "Would you like more?" he asked me.

"No," Jessalyn said, answering for me. "Cinder needs to help me freshen up for dinner."

I did as instructed. After that, I rushed around while she dined with the prince. I helped the guardsmen with the luggage, doing my best to swallow a few bites of dinner between trips up and down the stairs. I had to constantly rush to the dining room to attend to Jessalyn, who couldn't seem to let a moment pass without reminding the prince and me both of my true station.

Through it all, I saw the prince's puzzlement grow. I saw the way he scrutinized her, and the way he grew distant as she prattled on, alternately flattering him and assuring him what a wonderful wife she'd be.

Finally, the meal ended, and Jessalyn excused herself for the night. Xavier stood and kissed her hand. Then, as she made her way to the door, he turned to me. "Sit with me, Eldon," he said. "Help me finish this champagne."

His invitation made me grin "I'd love to," I said, sitting down in across from him in the chair my cousin had vacated.

But of course, Jessalyn couldn't bear to leave me with him. "I'm afraid I need Cinder with me."

"I thought you were going to bed," Xavier said, raising his eyebrows at her. "Certainly you don't require Eldon's assistance there?"

The suggestion caused Jess and me both to blush. "Of course not," Jessalyn said. "But I want to take a bath first. I need Cinder to haul up the water."

"I'm sure someone from the inn can assist you."

She put her shoulders back and flipped her hair back in defiance. "I won't allow strangers into my room."

Xavier's expression turned skeptical. He cocked his head back a bit. I knew he was debating whether to give in or not.

"Sire?" I was sitting directly across from him. By turning further toward him, putting my back to Jessalyn, I was able to grant us the illusion of privacy. I pitched my voice low, hoping she wouldn't be able to hear. "I'll find you later."

The smile that bloomed on his face was broad and beautiful. "I'd like that," he said, matching my hushed tone. What I saw in his eyes as he said it made the color rise on my cheeks. It made my heart leap inside my chest. It wasn't romantic, or suggestive. It was simply the sincerity of his desire to see me, and to spend time with me. It made me ache in a way that was both exhilarating and heartbreaking.

He was the wind, and I would take whatever little bit of him I could reach.

"Who do you think you are?" Jessalyn raged at me, once we were alone in her room. "Drinking champagne with him! Sitting at the table as if you were equals!"

"He invited me."

"It's pathetic!" she practically spat the word at me. "Here on the road, where there are only guards around, he may treat you like a friend, but once we're at the palace, he'll forget you. And then I'll send you home."

Her words stung, because there was a chance she was right. At the palace, he probably had other friends—men who really were his equal in every way. But there was no point in worrying about it, and there was even less point in arguing.

I ignored everything she said after that. I kept my head down and I did my job. She railed on, throwing barbs at me, telling me I was a fool, telling me I was nothing. I didn't say a word, and eventually she gave up on goading me.

When the bath was done and I'd hauled away the tub, I bid her good night and turned to leave.

"I didn't say you could go. I won't have you running off to tell the prince lies about me."

My grip on the doorknob tightened. My knuckles were white. "I know where I stand," I said through clenched teeth. "You made things quite clear today in the carriage."

"I still don't trust you."

"There doesn't seem to be much I can do about that."

"I could order you to stay."

My patience was at an end. Yes, I worked for her, but she didn't own me. I turned to face her. "I'm leaving," I said.

"Go ahead and yell. Go ahead and scream. Let the whole damn inn hear you rage. Do you really think that will help? Do you think the prince will think better of you when you're done?"

She opened her mouth to speak, but no sound came out. It seemed I'd finally struck her speechless. I did my best not to gloat as I left her.

I stood outside Xavier's door for a long time, willing my heart to stop racing. Trying to work up enough courage to knock.

The door opened before I had a chance.

"Eldon, what are you doing standing out here in the hallway? Come in, for heaven's sake!" He took my hand and pulled me inside, closing the door behind me. "I'm afraid I finished the champagne without you. Rude, I know, but it seemed the best way to kill the time."

"It's fine," I said. "I'm not really used to drinking anyway."

"Did she finally let you go?"

Not exactly, but it didn't seem worthwhile to go into it. "I think she's gone to bed."

He shook his head, turning away from me as if he couldn't bear to face me. "Do you think I'm crazy?" he asked.

"Why would I think that?"

"For marrying her?"

"Not crazy. Just…." I wasn't really sure how to finish my sentence. Misled? Taken by his faithful dog to the right house, but the wrong woman?

"Yes?" he prodded. "Go on. Tell me what you think."

What exactly could I say? "I think whatever happened at the ball must have made quite an impression."

"Yes. It was extraordinary." The fondness of the memory made his voice soft. "I wish I could tell you about that night and have you understand."

Of course I already knew all about that night, but the idea of hearing it from his perspective intrigued me. "Why wouldn't I?"

"It's only that it seems so crazy. It was...." He shook his head. "It was like magic."

I found myself smiling. "You don't believe in magic."

He laughed grudgingly. "I know." He pushed his hair back from his forehead and sighed. "But there was something about her. Something so *familiar.* Like I already knew her."

His words seemed to warm me from the inside. It *had* been magical.

"I kissed her." He glanced at me sideways, as if he expected me to disapprove.

"And?"

"It was like nothing else I've ever experienced. It was like coming home. It was...." He shook his head. "I can't describe it."

But I didn't need him to describe it. I remembered the taste of him, the feel of his lips against on mine, the tightness of his arms around me, the soft moan he'd made as we'd kissed. "It was amazing."

"Excuse me?"

His words shook me out of my reverie. He was staring at me in surprised amusement. "Oh." I'd been so lost in my memory of that night. I hadn't meant to speak at all. "I'm sorry. I didn't mean to be presumptuous."

He shook his head. "Don't apologize, Eldon. You're right. Everything about that night was amazing." He reached into his satchel. He pulled out the shoe and held it for me to see. It looked a bit worse for the wear. "I was ecstatic when I found this. Between it and Milton, I had a way to find her."

At the sound of his name, Milton rose from his place by the fire. He padded over to his master, his tail wagging.

Xavier held the shoe down to him. "Milton: find."

Milton took the shoe in his mouth. He plodded over to me and dropped the shoe at my feet.

Xavier shook his head with obvious confusion. "Maybe he's not such a good tracker after all."

"Well," I said shakily, "he led you to our house."

"To your marriageable cousin." His tone was lighthearted, and yet I knew it pained him.

"You don't want to marry her?"

"I want to marry the girl I danced with." He shook his head again. "The girl I kissed."

"You don't believe Jessalyn is that girl?"

He moaned in frustration. "I don't know. I suppose she must be. Milton led me to her. She's the right height. Her hair is as I remember. Her face.... Well, the lighting in the ballroom was poor, and I'd already danced with more than a dozen girls, and I'll admit I'd had a glass or two of champagne. It *must* be her. And yet...."

"And yet?" I prodded, when I realized he didn't intend to go on.

"I thought that when I saw her, it would be as magical as it was at the ball. That I'd recognize her immediately, like being struck by lightning."

"But it wasn't."

"Not even close."

He sat down on the one chair in the room, his elbows on his knees and his head in his hands. I'd never seen him so beaten.

I had to tell him the truth. Whatever Jessalyn had said to me in the carriage was irrelevant. I couldn't lie to him any longer. I was terrified—my heart hammered painfully inside my chest, and my palms began to sweat—but I knew it was the right thing to do.

"Sire?" My voice shook. "What if I told you that you're right? That Jessalyn isn't the right girl."

He looked up at me, his eyes bright with hope. "You know who she is?"

I do. That's what I tried to say, but the words wouldn't come out. He was watching me expectantly, and I forced myself to nod.

"Go on."

"This will sound crazy, but—"

"For heaven's sake, Eldon, tell me!"

I took a deep breath and said, "It was me. I traded the fish you left me to the witch, and she turned me into a girl for one night so I'd have a chance to say goodbye."

My words seemed to echo in the silence. He was surprised at first, but it quickly gave way to confusion, and then his eyes hardened in a way I'd never seen before. "I suppose you think that's funny," he said as he stood up and turned away from me. "It's easy for you to joke. It's not your life."

He didn't believe me. Of course he didn't. Why would he? It was utterly absurd.

I opened my mouth to speak. I could convince him. I could recount that evening, and the dance, and the conversation we'd had. That's all it would take.

But then I thought forward to what would come once he *did* believe me.

He could not marry me. The girl he longed for would still be gone. Jessalyn was right about one thing: if he chose not to marry her, we'd likely both be sent away, and he'd be forever out of my reach. I'd never see him again. The thought caused my breath to catch in my throat.

I couldn't bear to leave him now.

If he married Jess, I'd at least be with him. I'd still have his friendship. My temporary resolve to tell him the truth died in my chest. Being with him in any capacity was more important to me.

"I'm sorry, Sire," I said, deliberately using a title instead of his name. "I shouldn't have made light of the situation. I was only trying to make you laugh."

He took a deep breath and let it out in a rush. His shoulders fell, and when he turned to face at me, he was almost smiling. "Don't call me 'Sire.'"

"Yes, Sire."

He laughed sheepishly. "You won't tell her what I've said, will you?"

He could have ordered me not to speak of it. Instead, he was asking for my silence. Asking me to keep his secret, as if we were equals. Asking as my friend. "I would never betray you." I wondered if he could hear my love for him in those few words.

He crossed the room to put his hand on my shoulder. He looked down into my eyes. "You're a good friend, Eldon," he said. "It will be worth marrying your cousin to keep you near."

I ducked my head so he would so he wouldn't see how his words affected me. I didn't know if the feeling welling up inside my chest was joy or anguish. I didn't know if I should laugh or cry. My eyes ached with unshed tears, and I shut them tight in effort to keep them at bay.

It would be worth seeing her married to him, if it allowed me moments like this.

We arrived at the palace the next day. Jessalyn and I were each assigned rooms. I was surprised to find that mine wasn't in the servant quarters as I'd expected, but in the main wing. It was vast and sumptuous. The curtains were velvet and the sheets were made of silk. It was luxurious to the extreme. Jessalyn was outraged when she found out, mostly because I was closer to Xavier than she was. I knew it annoyed it her to no end. The entirety of my worldly possessions only filled one drawer of the massive armoire. I felt completely out of place.

My assumption that the prince had peers at the palace was quickly dispelled. True, there was a large group of young men and women who attempted to follow him and dote on him and catch his attention, but he managed to avoid them more often than not.

"They're not my friends," he told me, when I referred to them as such. "They'd each throw me to the wolves in a minute, if I wasn't my father's son."

For his part, Xavier seemed to have resigned himself to marriage. He spent most of his time with Jessalyn, planning the wedding.

Jessalyn's resolve to keep me away from the prince was stronger than ever. She kept me busy from dawn until dusk. She sent me on errands that kept me running from one end of the palace to the other. She sent me to town, sometimes three times in a day. She sent servants to find me and issue orders. Several times the orders were to undo what I'd just spent the whole morning doing. There was no rhyme or reason to her instructions, save one: keep me from Xavier. And at that, she succeeded, for a few days at least.

Late on the fourth day, I returned from town with a new shawl Jessalyn had commissioned just as she and Xavier were finishing dinner.

"It's absolutely the wrong size," she said when I showed it to her. "And I specifically told her to use the green, not the blue. Take it back at once."

I barely even heard her. I couldn't take my eyes off the prince.

He was smiling at me, that bright infectious smile that made me feel like I could fly.

"It's good to finally see you, Eldon. How have you been?"

I've missed your face and your voice and our afternoons fishing. I miss hearing you laugh. I'd given anything to have you to myself, if only for an hour. But I couldn't say any of that. Instead, I took a deep breath and said, "I'm good, Sire. Thank you for asking. It's wonderful to see you."

He lowered his eyebrow at me in a playful scowl. "Don't call me 'Sire.'"

"Yes, Sire."

The corner of his mouth twitched in amusement. "You look well."

"Thank you, Sire. Xavier. So do you." It was a lie, though. He *didn't* look well at all. The smile he gave me appeared to be genuine, but the one he turned on Jessalyn was fake. I could see the strain of the impending marriage in the tightness of his shoulders and the dark circles under his eyes.

He was obviously miserable.

"Cinder," Jessalyn said, shoving the shawl back into my hands, "this is unacceptable. Take it back now. Tell her I won't put up with shoddy work. If she can't do it right, I'll take my business someplace else."

Did she see the way the prince frowned at her? Did she see the way his expression darkened with disapproval?

"Surely it can wait until morning," he said.

She shook her head. "I intended to wear this to the engagement party the day after tomorrow," she said. "It's her own fault for getting it wrong."

And so I took myself back to town to inform the poor seamstress that my cousin had changed her mind about both the size and color, but was too arrogant to admit it.

The next day, I had a plan. I scheduled my tasks well. I timed everything perfectly. I picked up the new shawl early, but waited until the prince's dinner with Jessalyn was ending to present it. I let myself quietly through the dining room door. They were talking, and neither of them seemed to notice me.

"I can't believe they served us fish," Jessalyn complained.

Xavier blinked at her, clearly trying to maintain an expression of polite interest. "I requested it," he said. "I was under the impression you liked it."

"Certainly not. Your father's right. It's peasant food."

"But I thought you liked fishing?" he said. "At the ball, you said—"

"I have your new shawl," I said, stepping forward and cutting off the disastrous conversation. Jessalyn looked up at me with obvious annoyance. And Xavier?

He smiled at me again, as he had the day before. It seemed to warm me, all the way to my toes.

"Two days in a row, Eldon," he said. "We might make a habit out of this."

Jessalyn snatched the shawl from my hands and inspected it. "I suppose it will do," she said.

"I think it's lovely," Xavier said to her. "The color suits you."

She batted her eyes at him, simpering. I envisioned ripping her hair out of her pretty head. "Thank you, Xavier."

He winced when she said his name, although he hid it by wiping his face with his napkin. "Well," he said, putting the linen down and pushing his chair back. "I think I'll bid you good night." He stood. She held her hand out to him, and he took it and dutifully kissed the back of it.

Then he turned to me.

"Eldon, will you join me for a drink?"

I tried to keep my expression neutral, lest Jessalyn see my happiness and try to thwart me. But this was what I'd hoped for. This was the reason I'd planned my day so carefully, waiting until after dinner to find him. I'd hoped he'd have a few moments to spend with me. "I'd love to—" I started to say. But of course Jessalyn cut me off.

"He can't," she said. "I need him to prepare my bath."

She was still seated at the table, and when Xavier turned to face her, I could see how little patience he had left for her.

"I'm sure somebody else can assist you."

"You know how I feel about letting strangers into my room."

"This is your home now," he said. "They're not strangers. They're servants, and they're paid to serve."

"I don't know who to ask—"

"Find. Somebody. Else."

"Yes, but Cinder is *my* servant."

His jaw clenched. He took a deep breath and said with the still calmness of barely controlled rage, "He's more than your servant. He's your cousin. And he's *my* friend."

"Surely you have other friends—"

She might have slapped him, his reaction was so sudden and so strong. He pulled himself up to his full height and looked down at her with disdain. "I am your future husband," he said, his voice like ice. "More than that, I am your prince. I desire an hour or two with your *servant*. Is that *really* too much to ask? It costs you nothing. Are you truly unable to grant me such a simple request?"

She stared up at him with wide eyes. She had gambled, and she had lost, and now she had pushed him too far. I could see her sorting through her options, trying to decide how to appease him. But whatever she was to do, he had no interest in hearing it.

"With me, Eldon," he said.

It wasn't a request. It was an order. Possibly the first he'd ever given me. I had no choice but to follow. He was a river, and I was a leaf caught in his current. I let him carry me out the door. Down the hall.

Away from Jessalyn.

His anger faded quickly once we were in the hall. He sighed heavily. "I'm sorry you had to see that," he said. "I'm sorry you have to be involved."

"It's not your fault."

"It feels like it is. This whole damn mess is because of me."

"I could say the same thing about myself," I said. Or *Jessalyn*.

"I've missed you."

It wasn't sentimental. It wasn't shy. It was said with the same casual sincerity he might use to say, "The sky is blue," or "The sun is bright." There was no embarrassment and no apology. Only a simple statement of fact.

"I've missed you, too," I said. And I knew I'd failed to sound as casual as he.

We reached his room and he led me inside. Milton jumped off the bed with a howl and launched himself at me. His massive forepaws landed on my chest, and I fell back against the door as he tried to lick my face.

"Milton, off!" Xavier scolded.

Milton sighed and dropped dutifully to all four paws. I scratched his ears as a reward.

"I guess he missed you, too," Xavier said as he removed his dinner jacket and tossed it onto his bed. He gestured at a sumptuous armchair near the door. "Have a seat. Relax."

I followed the first order, and attempted to follow the second. The chair was deep and soft, and I could almost have slept in it. Milton turned and disappeared through a door into what must have been Xavier's closet.

"I should have brought some champagne," Xavier said. "Or some wine."

"It's fine. I don't usually drink."

"You keep saying that. I intend to change it." He ran his hands through his hair and scowled. "Frankly, I'd love to get drunk enough to forget this impending marriage, if only for a night."

I wasn't sure there was enough alcohol in the world for that, but I didn't answer. He didn't seem to be in the mood for jokes.

Milton emerged from the closet. He had something in his mouth. He looked quite determined, even for a dog. He plodded straight over to me and dropped his prize in my lap.

It was the shoe.

"Milton," Xavier scolded with obvious exasperation. "What is it with you and that slipper?"

Milton cocked his head at his master, as if to say, "What do you mean?"

"Oh, that damn thing!" Xavier swore, turning away to put his head in his hands. "If I hadn't found it, I wouldn't be in this mess."

"You'd still be getting married."

He sighed and scrubbed his hands over his face. "I suppose you're right, but at least it would have been a girl of my choosing. But now…."

"You still doubt she's the right girl."

He reached down and took the shoe from me, staring at it as if it held the answer. "I don't just 'doubt,' Eldon. I *know*. Everything about her is wrong: the way she laughs and the way she tries to flatter me and the way she bats her eyelashes and the things she says, and the way she—" He stopped short, and I knew there was something else.

"Yes?" I prompted. "And what?"

He turned to look at me. His cheeks were red. "The way she tastes," he said, his voice quiet. "I know that sounds crude, but I kissed her. I wanted to see if it felt like it did that night."

"But it didn't?"

"No. Not even close."

I didn't know what to say. All the questions that had plagued me since the day Jessalyn had slipped her foot into the shoe were running circles in my mind. Should I try once again to tell him? Would he believe me? What good could it possibly do anyway?

"Damn it all," he swore in frustration, throwing himself backward onto his bed. He glared again at the slipper in his hand. "How could this have happened, Eldon? How could it have gone so wrong?" He sat up and pointed the shoe at me. "She ran, as if the devil himself were after her. I chased her out the door, and I found this. I gave it to Milton." He looked down at Milton, who glared at him with barely disguised disgust. "He's supposed to be the finest tracking dog in the kingdom. When I gave it to him, he gave all the signs of having the trail, but...." He stopped, staring down forlornly at the shoe. "He led me straight to your house, Eldon. Straight to Jessalyn."

No, not to Jessalyn. To me. But how could I tell him that?

"Milton, come."

Milton went obediently to his master.

Xavier held the shoe out to Milton. "Milton: find."

Milton huffed. He took the slipper in his heavy, wet jowls. He padded across the room. He dropped the sodden thing in my lap, then turned his mournful doggy gaze to the prince.

"Every time!" Xavier said, laughing bitterly. "Every time, he leads me straight to you! It makes no sense! It's as if...."

He stopped, his expression going from confused to contemplative. "As if...."

He stared at me, lost in thought.

"Straight to you," he said again.

My heart raced. My palms were suddenly damp. He stood up, staring at me, his eyes full of wonder and surprise. My mouth went dry.

"Your eyes," he said, his voice barely a whisper.

I ducked my head, suddenly unable to stand the weight of his gaze upon me. I didn't know if I wanted him to discover the truth or not. I hated lying to him, but if he knew Jessalyn was the wrong person, he'd refuse to marry her. He'd choose another bride, and I'd lose him.

"Look at me," he said, giving me an order for the second time that night. It took every ounce of my will to obey. His intensity was disconcerting. I couldn't think. I could barely breathe. He stepped up to my seat and held his hand down to me. "Dance with me."

I had to force myself to speak. "Sire?" My voice didn't sound right at all. It was entirely too rough, and too shaky.

"You heard me," he said. "Dance with me."

I rose, although my knees shook. He took my right hand in his left. He put his arm around my waist. It made my heart race, being so close to him again. "Are you ready?" he asked.

"No."

"Yes, you are," he said. "Now."

He started to dance. It should have been easy. He was leading. I had only to follow. But I failed. The first step I managed to fake. The second, I went the wrong way, but corrected quickly. The third, I went forward when I should have gone back, and we ran into each other.

"Again," he said, but I'd lost any semblance of grace. As soon as he started to move again, I stumbled and nearly fell, stepping on his foot in the process.

"Eldon, what are you doing?"

"I don't know how to dance."

Only a few words, yet the change they caused him was profound. He was shocked, and hurt. "But…." He let me go, backing up a step, obviously confused. "That can't be."

I didn't know what to say, and I watched as he went from confused to defeated, his eyes going dark, his shoulders slumping. "Sire?"

"Stop calling me that!"

"Xavier—" But before I could say more, he waved my words away.

"I'm sorry," he said, turning away from me. "I was being a fool. I don't know what I was thinking."

But I *did* know what he'd been thinking, and the infuriating thing was, he'd been right. I'd tried to tell him once, but he hadn't believed me. I still didn't know what I had to gain by convincing him of the truth, but I hated to see him so lost. I wanted to touch him. I longed to dance with him again, even if it meant tripping over my own feet. I wanted him to look at me with that bright, astounded expression.

"It was the magic," I said.

It was barely a whisper. It was a miracle he heard me, but he did.

He turned to me, his eyes wide. "That's what she said, when I complimented her dancing."

"I know."

He didn't answer, but I could tell he was considering it again, replaying the night in his mind, trying to decide if it was possible. He stepped closer. He put his finger under my chin and tilted my head back, forcing me to meet his eyes. He used his other hand on the small of my back to pull me closer. "Could it be?" he asked.

Yes! I wanted to cry. *Yes, it could be, and it is!* But before I could answer, he kissed me.

His lips were soft. His touch was light. It was just as it had been on the dance floor—my legs shaking and unsteady, the gentleness of his hand on my back. The surety that I was only still standing because he held me up. I put my arms around his neck and opened myself up to him. His tongue touched my lips, testing—*tasting*—and I whimpered. He moaned in response, putting both of his arms around me, pulling me tight against him, kissing me deeper.

This was how it should be—chest to chest, not with the strange sensation of breasts pressed between us, but as two men, groin to groin, the proof his arousal hard against me. When he pulled back to look at me, his eyes were full of wonder.

"It *is* you!"

"I tried to tell you. I only wanted to see you again. I missed you that day in the woods, and I just wanted to say goodbye." The words spilled out of me, tumbling over each other in their haste to finally be free. "The witch did the spell, but I never meant for any of this to happen. I never expected you to choose me. I just wanted one dance. I didn't want you to leave without seeing you one last time. And so I went to the ball, and we were dancing, and it was all so perfect, but then the spell wore off, and I had to leave in such a hurry, and I lost the shoe. And then you showed up the next day with Milton, and I had no idea what to do."

"Why didn't you tell me?"

"I tried to, that night at the inn, but you didn't believe me. And I was so worried you'd send me away. I can't bear for you to send me away, Xavier. Please let me stay—"

He kissed me, cutting off my breathless plea. There was no hesitation. Only urgency. His kiss was a demand. An order. His fingers fumbled at the buttons on my shirt, and then my belt. He pushed me back on the bed. Part of me worried having this much of him now would only make it hurt more when I lost him, but I had no power to resist him. I was overwhelmed, as I so often was in his presence, the sheer force of his will propelling me forward, carrying me where he wanted me to be. I could only cling to him and trust he'd see me safely to the other side. I was lost in him—the weight of him on top of me, the way he tasted, the sounds he made, the softness of his lips, and insistence of his hands.

Lord, his *hands*.

They seemed to be everywhere, touching and teasing, and just when I thought the pleasure must surely peak and burn out, he'd shift his focus, touch me someplace new, ignite some yet unknown spark of desire within me, fanning it into a flame, stoking it into a wildfire that burned me up and consumed me.

When it was over, we lay spent and breathless, the sticky wetness of our pleasure cooling between us. His arms were tight around me, his face buried in my neck. I was glad he couldn't see the dampness on my cheeks.

"Eldon," he whispered, "what in the world are we going to do?"

3

I slept there with him, his arms tight around me as if he thought I might try to escape. Not that I had any intention of doing so. It was a peacefulness I had never known, curled up against his strong body, the brush of his breath on the back of my neck. Knowing he cared for me, on some level at least.

He woke me once in the night, rousing me from the depths of slumber, raising me again to the heights of pleasure. His mouth was warm and sweet and his hands were gentle yet insistent. He was firm in his desire. I could not have told him no. And yet what he seemed to want most was to please me.

I wished morning would never come. There was no price I wouldn't have paid for a magic that would have let my night with him last forever. But it was not to be.

I woke to the bells of the tower. It was six o'clock. The glow of morning sunlight through the curtains made the room feel soft and somehow secretive. Xavier was already up, sitting in the chair I'd occupied the night before, watching me. He didn't say a word.

For the first time, I felt awkward with him. He had a robe on, but I was still naked. I was painfully aware of the tan lines on my skin—most of my body was pale, but my arms, face and the back of my neck were bronze, betraying the hours I'd spent working in the sun. I hated the callouses on my hands. I was ashamed of my often-patched clothes as I hurriedly pulled them on. His silence seemed ominous.

I finally turned to face him. A billion questions and hopes and worries stormed through my mind. Did he regret it? Did he want to see me again? Was it a one-time thing? I didn't even know how to leave. Was I to be kissed, as his lover? Bid goodbye, as a friend? Or excused, like a servant? Or worse, like a whore?

I could tell nothing by his eyes.

"Sire?" I wished my voice didn't shake. I wished I still felt as sure with him as I had before he'd taken me to his bed.

He smiled at me, but only a barely. It was a thin, sad smile. "Don't call me that."

"Xavier—"

He stood suddenly, cutting me off. "I'll break off the engagement today."

My heart stopped beating. I could barely make myself breathe, let alone speak. His words felt like the end of everything I'd hoped for. "Why?"

"*Why?*" His voice was hard and bitter, and I instinctively took a step back. "Why do you think?"

"You have to take a wife—"

"She's not the girl I want!" He stepped closer to me. His anger gave way to something gentle. He brushed his fingers over my cheek. "She's not the one I love."

If my heart had stopped beating before, it kicked into high speed now. "You love me?"

He smiled at me. He put his arms around me and pulled me close. "Eldon, you have no idea how many times I wanted to touch you, or to kiss you, but I was afraid you'd be horrified. If I'd only known…." He kissed my neck. His hand caressed my back. "Now that I do, we can be together. The way we should be."

A ridiculous, giddy grin threatened my composure. But I knew he wasn't seeing the whole picture.

"And what about your crown?"

He froze, his lips still against the pounding pulse in my neck, and I knew I was right. He hadn't thought it through. "Who cares?" he said at last. "I don't need it."

"So you'll give up your title and your inheritance? Leave the palace? Renounce your claim to your family's money and all the luxuries that go with it?"

I was challenging him now, and he took a step back, standing up straight, putting his shoulders back, the way he always did when somebody questioned his authority. "Yes. Why not?"

"Have you thought about what that would be like?"

"I don't need to. All that matters is that we'd be together."

The fact that he'd consider giving up his title for me was astounding. It made my heart swell inside my chest. It made me feel like I could fly.

But I knew he'd regret it in the end.

"What would we do? Live in my aunt's house, both of us as servants? I'm not even paid a salary."

His certainty began to fade as he considered my words. "Then we'll leave."

"And go where? What would you have us do? It's true, I could find a spot in another house. You could find work as a clerk maybe, or a tutor. We might make enough between us to get a room in town, at a boarding house. Is that what you want? To live like a peasant?" My words hurt him. I could see it. But he had to consider the consequences of his rash decisions. "No more horses. No more afternoons spent playing fetch with Milton. No more custom riding boots or exquisite meals. No more champagne that tastes like sunlight." That statement seemed to confuse him, but I rushed on. "No money. No title. Nothing. I'm glad you like fish, Xavier, because we'd be eating it nearly every day. Is that how you want to live? Do I mean so much to you as that?"

He wilted—there was no other way to put it. He slumped down into his chair with his head in his hands.

"What do you suggest?"

"Marry her," I said. "Marry anyone. Take the wife your father's law demands." He looked up at me, shock and disbelief in his eyes. "Only...." My voice caught, and I had to take a deep breath before I could go on. "Only let me stay. That's all I ask. Don't send me away."

"And then what, Eldon? Hide you away like some dark secret while she enjoys the prestige of being my wife?"

"I don't care about prestige. The only thing I care about is being with you in whatever capacity you'll have me."

It was pathetic, I knew, the depths I was willing to sink to just to keep some small piece of him, but my words made him smile—a bright, joyous smile that made his whole face light up. He stood up and took my hand, pulling me into his arms. "Don't you see? That's why you deserve it more than her."

He kissed me. He was so solid and so sure. I slid my hands inside his robe, sighing at the warmth of his smooth skin against my fingers. I could feel that power welling up in him, making his kisses harder and his touch insistent. It threatened to ignite a fire in both of us that would quickly make me forget my duties. But before it could sweep me away, we were interrupted by a knock at the door.

I was still trying to catch my breath when Xavier answered it.

It was a servant—a young boy I didn't know, who glanced with obvious curiosity between the prince in his robe and me. "Sire, the Lady Jessalyn sent me to find Cinder."

"Where were you?" Jessalyn snapped as I entered her room. "I've had the servants looking everywhere for you!"

"He was with the prince," the servant volunteered. I resisted the urge to kick his feet from under him.

Jessalyn turned her disdainful gaze my way. "First you disgrace me at dinner, then you rush off to bother him before he even has breakfast." She turned away from me to regard herself in the mirror once more. She brushed powder over her nose. "I've seen the way you look at him. It's disgusting. I hate to think what he'll say if he ever finds out how you feel about him."

I turned away, not because I couldn't bear to face her, but because I didn't want her to see how her words made me smile. In the past, as recently as a day ago, her words would have stung, but not now. Instead, I thought of him. I thought of the way he'd held me. The way he'd touched me. I thought of the soft brush of his fingers against my cheeks, and the gentleness in his voice as he'd said, "She's not the one I love."

She could not hurt me. Whatever happened, my fate was no longer tied to hers. Maybe he'd marry her and maybe he wouldn't. Either way, I felt sure he'd allow me to stay.

Jessalyn was still talking. I was vaguely aware of her—not of her actual words, but of her tone—so petulant and disdainful. So arrogant.

I ignored her, and I called up in my mind the feel of him on top of me. The taste of him as he kissed me. The warmth of his mouth on the most intimate parts of me. I couldn't help but smile.

"Cinder, are you even listening?"

"Of course," I said. It was a lie, but it didn't matter.

She held her hairbrush out to me. "I'm having breakfast with him in half an hour," she said. "I need you to do my hair the way he likes."

I could have told her no. I could have walked away. But her shallow, self-centered venom couldn't touch me now. The memory of my night with him was like a still, quiet pool between Jessalyn and me. If she shouted, I might hear, but she couldn't touch me. She couldn't shatter the gentle joy he'd given me.

I brushed her hair, and she prattled on. She talked of the seamstress making the wedding gown, of which the ruffles were old-fashioned and unflattering. She talked of the servants, who all moved too slowly. She talked of the cake baker, who used too much cream in her frosting. She talked of the endless ways in which the world did not meet her exacting standards.

And through it all, I felt his touch on my skin.

Finally, she was ready to meet the prince. She left for breakfast, and I was sent to town to purchase a particular bath oil she simply couldn't live without.

I took my time. It was a gorgeous day. I felt light and free and somehow reborn. Part of me wanted to worry about what would happen next, but I chose to ignore it. I refused to let doubt darken my mood. For now, the memory of my night with him was enough. I wandered aimlessly through the market, smiling like a fool as I thought of him. I could still taste his kisses. I could smell him on my skin. It seemed like all I would ever need.

Eventually though, soft morning sunlight gave way to the bright, hot light of midday, and I admitted to myself I couldn't live in my memories forever. It was time to go back. It was almost lunchtime, and Jessalyn would undoubtedly be looking for me, ready to send me off on some brand new errand.

I knew something was wrong as soon as I returned. The halls of the palace seemed unusually hushed. Servants whispered together in corners. They glanced at me nervously as I passed.

As I neared Jessalyn's room, I heard shouting. When I rounded the corner, I found myself facing half a dozen guards. A couple seemed uncomfortable. Most were clearly amused. And in their midst was Jessalyn.

Her face was red. Her hands were balled into fists at her side. The hair I'd so carefully styled for her that morning was in disarray, hanging in a tangled mess down her back.

As soon as she saw me, she flew at me in a rage. "This is your fault!" she screamed. "You did this to me!"

The guard nearest me caught her before she reached me, grabbing her around the waist.

"Don't touch me!" she yelled, turning to pound his armored chest with her fists. He stood there, solid and unmoving, looking like he was having a hell of a time not bursting out laughing.

"My Lady," one of the others said, stepping forward. He had red braids on his shoulders, which I'd learned meant he was a captain. "Our orders are to escort you from the palace grounds."

"What?" I asked, stunned. "They're kicking us out?"

Nobody answered me. I wasn't sure they'd even heard me. They were too busy focusing on Jessalyn.

"You're leaving," the captain said to her, calm and rational. "It's that simple. The choice is yours: you can go peacefully, or you can make a scene. It matters little to us."

The one who'd kept her from attacking me laughed. "We'll haul you out kicking and screaming, if we have to."

She turned to glare at him. "You wouldn't dare!"

He grinned wickedly at her. "Try me."

I felt as if I'd been kicked in the stomach. After what had happened last night, Xavier was kicking us out? I couldn't believe it. I left Jessalyn to her fate and went in search of the man I loved.

The man who said he loved me back.

At his door, I found the same young servant who had interrupted us that very morning. He was sitting on the floor, leaning against Xavier's door, but as soon as he saw me, he scrambled to his feet.

"He told me to wait here for you, sir," he said. He pulled a piece of paper from his pocket and held it out to me. "He said to make sure you got this."

The note was short. It said only:

There's something I must do. I'll be back in three days. Trust me.
Love — X

Nothing else.

I turned the paper over, stupidly hoping to find more on the back, but there was nothing there.

"I don't understand," I said, more to myself than to the young servant. "Where did he go? Why are they kicking us out?"

The boy shook his head. "Not you, sir," he said. "Only the lady."

"Not me?"

He shook his head again. "Everybody's talking about it, sir. They say he specifically said not to let the lady take you."

"Who's everybody?"

"The servants, sir." He grinned at me. "We hear lots, you know."

Of course I knew. I was one.

"And what about the wedding?" It was scheduled to take place in only three days.

"It's still on, sir. They say he specifically told them he'd be back in time."

The wedding was still on, and yet Jessalyn was being kicked out? "Stop calling me sir," I said.

"Yes, sir."

I sighed. I had a renewed sympathy for Xavier. "Where did he go?"

"Nobody knows for sure, sir, but the rumor is, he went back."

"Back where?"

"Back to your town," he said. "Back to where you're from."

If that was true, time was short. The trip from my home had taken us two days, although we'd been moving at the speed of the carriage. Alone on horseback, it was possible he could make it there and back in time for the wedding, but there'd be little time to spare. "Why is he going there?"

"They say he picked the wrong girl."

The wrong girl?

"They say the prince meant to pick her twin, but Jessalyn locked her sister in the closet and tricked the prince into taking her instead."

It was absurd. After all, I knew Penelope wasn't the right girl any more than Jess was. I also knew Jess hadn't done anything as drastic as locking her sister in the closet. On the other hand, I sure wouldn't have put it past her if it had come to that.

Was it was possible Xavier had decided to go through with the marriage, but had decided Penelope was the better choice? She was, after all, not nearly so conniving. If I had to see him wed to one of my marriageable cousins, I certainly would have chosen Penelope over Jess.

Still, it made no sense.

"Is there anything else?" I asked.

The boy grinned at me and leaned closer as if sharing a remarkable secret. "Only that nobody's too sorry to see her go." He straightened back up and made a noticeable effort to stop smiling. It didn't quite work. "That's all," he said. "Sir."

The next few days were the strangest of my life. For the first time in years, nobody was giving me orders. I had no duties. No chores. I had absolutely nothing to do.

Jessalyn was gone. The rumors said she had indeed been carried kicking and screaming out of the palace. The guards deposited her just outside the gate. They say she stayed there for several hours, yelling and pleading and doing her best to convince anybody who would listen that it was all a horrible mistake. Eventually, the guards tired of jeering at her. They resorted to pelting her with dirt clods. When those ran out, they threatened horse dung. After that, she gave up and wandered away. She was never heard from again.

I didn't miss her.

I quickly found idleness didn't suit me, and of course there was plenty of work to be done. The palace was bordering on chaos. There was still a wedding to be planned, albeit with no bride and no groom. Xavier's mother took over, and preparations resumed in earnest. Nobody knew what to do about the bride's dress, but other than that, things were much as they had been before, except without Jessalyn's constant complaints.

The eve of Xavier's birthday dawned warm and bright and beautiful. It was the day of the wedding. The ceremony was planned for late in the evening, due to some ancient custom I knew nothing about. A feast was to be served after. The servants were busy, but not too busy to gossip.

The prince was home. Or maybe he wasn't. He'd brought a bride. Or maybe he hadn't. It all depended on who you asked. Some said he'd rescued a princess from a tower, but whether he'd done so by climbing her hair or by defeating a dragon or both was up for debate. I followed the gossip obsessively for the first few hours, desperate for word of Xavier, but eventually I realized it was pointless. Xavier would return home at some point, with or without a bride. I would learn the truth of it all eventually. Worrying about it now would only drive me insane.

After that, I bent my head to my work and did my best to ignore the gossip.

The day passed in a frantic blur of activity. When sunset came, I was in the dining room, helping set the many tables.

"Eldon Cinder!"

The voice rang through the dining room like a bell. Complete silence fell as everybody turned toward the door. It was one of the guards. "Is Eldon Cinder here?" he asked again.

Everybody turned my way. I cleared my throat and made myself speak. "I'm Eldon."

"You're to come with me."

He didn't wait to see if I was following. He simply turned and strode purposefully away. I had to hurry to catch up.

"Where are we going?" I asked as I jogged along behind him through the palace corridor.

"To the wedding."

"Has the prince returned?"

"He has. Not more than five minutes ago. Went straight to the wedding in his riding clothes."

"Am I in some kind of trouble?"

"I don't know."

"But what—"

He stopped dead in his tracks, turning to face me. It happened so fast, I almost ran into him. "I don't know, sir. The prince told me to bring you. So I am. That's all."

Off he went again, and I rushed to keep up—right to the door of the cavernous palace courtroom.

I stopped there in the entry, looking up the aisle. Guests were seated on each side, dressed in their finest garb. I was suddenly horribly aware of my own clothes, faded and patched and dirty from the work I'd done through the day.

On the dais at the head of the room stood a flock of confused clerks, their long dark robes matching their long beards and dour expressions. The disapproval on their faces was evident. Next to them stood Xavier's parents, the king and queen. The king was baffled. The queen seemed intrigued. And in front of them all was Xavier, wearing the broadest smile I'd ever seen.

"Eldon!" Xavier called when he saw me. The room was so big, he practically had to yell. "Where were you?"

Everybody turned in their seats to stare at me, and I felt myself blush. "I was folding napkins."

Xavier laughed. The audience buzzed.

"Well," the prince said, "are you going to come up here, or will you make me wait all night?"

Walking up the aisle was the hardest thing I've ever done. My knees shook. My palms were damp. On each side of me there were faces, wide eyes staring at me as I passed. There were hushed whispers and people straining to see me past those who were seated along the aisle.

And then, finally there in front of me, was Xavier, as handsome and regal as ever, even in his rumpled riding clothes.

"Xav—Excellency?"

He smiled at my near-blunder, but all he said was, "Take off your shoe."

Behind me, a wave of whispers ran through the crowd, along with a few nervous chuckles.

"My shoe?" I asked stupidly.

"Yes," he said. "The right one."

I used my left foot to toe my worn right boot off. Xavier reached into the pocket of his velvet jacket and pulled out....

The shoe.

It bore little resemblance to the lacy, delicate sandal I'd worn to the ball. Milton had drooled on it a good deal over the past few days, and Xavier had clearly had to squish it to get it into his pocket.

He held it out to me. "Put it on."

Was this some kind of joke? "It won't fit."

"I think it will."

"I'm telling you, it won't. My foot is too big."

He leaned forward to whisper in my ear. "You're not the only one who leaves gifts for the witch," he said.

Of course. The witch.

I found myself smiling. The rumors had been true—he had gone back. But not to get Penelope.

"What did you give her?"

He grinned at me. "A whole box of mice." I couldn't tell if he was serious or not. He knelt in front of me and held the shoe for me to slip on.

I still didn't know exactly what was going on. The whole thing seemed crazy. But he was the prince. More than that, he was the man I loved, and he was on his knees in front of me, in front of his parents, in front of a court full of people, waiting for me to trust him.

I slipped my toes in. That should have been as much as I could manage. The ball of my foot shouldn't have gone past the straps.

But it did.

Somehow, my foot slipped inside. It wasn't that the shoe fit my foot. It was that suddenly, my foot fit the shoe. As Xavier stood up, watching me expectantly, I realized why he'd gone back to see the witch.

There, in front of everybody, amidst startled gasps and gaping mouths, the magic took hold. The tingling warmth of it spread up from my foot, over my ankles, up my thighs. I felt the changes again as they happened—hips widening, shoulders narrowing, hair growing, the structure of my face changing. One minute I was wearing my tattered clothes, a worn boot on one foot and a ridiculously ornate slipper that by all rights was way too small on the other, and the next moment I wore a woman's dress. It was long and white, tight and binding around my rib cage and breasts, billowing around my hips, full and heavy around my legs. On my feet, I still wore one boot and one lady's shoe, but they were hidden by the fullness of the skirt, and the magic somehow kept me from hobbling gracelessly on the uneven heels.

The crowd seemed to gasp as one, and then, there was utter silence.

I met Xavier's smiling eyes. "There's the girl I've been looking for," he said.

He held his hand out to me.

I wanted to take it, and yet, I wanted to know what this new magic entailed. Was I to remain like this? I hadn't wanted to be a woman to begin with. I certainly didn't want it to become a regular occurrence.

He must have seen the hesitation on my face, because he smiled. "Trust me."

Outside, the clock began to chime.

"You're almost out of time," the king said.

I took Xavier's hand

His smile grew, and he turned to the clerk. "We're ready." The clock chimed again, and he added, "Make it fast."

The clerk's shocked expression might have made me laugh if I hadn't been so worried about hyperventilating from nerves. The only thing that kept me together was Xavier—the strength of his hand holding mine. The sheer joy I saw shining in his eyes as he looked at me. The surety that this was what he wanted.

The ceremony was a blur. I must have said, "I do." The clock continued its slow, melodic chime. And then the clerk declared, "You now are joined as man and umm...wife?" He cleared his throat nervously. "You may kiss your bride."

And just as the twelfth chime rang out, Xavier kissed me. It wasn't romantic. It wasn't passionate. It was nothing more than a chaste, quick touch against my lips.

That worried me, but his eyes begged me to trust him. He squeezed my hand, assuring me it would be fine.

The spectators cheered, but Xavier turned toward them, holding up his hands to call for silence. They quieted quickly, and Xavier turned to his father.

"You agree I've met the requirement?" he asked. "I've taken a wife before my birthday?"

His father looked startled, but he nodded. "You have."

Xavier turned to the clerk. "Declare me heir to the kingdom."

There was a hustle of robed clerks, and a circlet was brought forward. It took forever. I stood there, my knees shaking, my heart in my throat, wondering what would happen next. There were speeches, and Xavier swore oath after oath. Finally, with much ceremony and overly-wordy oration, just as the clock struck one, the circlet was placed upon his brow, and he was declared Heir Confirmed to His Majesty's Kingdom, Crown Prince of the Land.

This time, there was no cheering. The crowd seemed to be waiting for him to make a speech.

"The law says I must take a wife before my birthday," he declared, his voice strong and pitched to carry to the far corners of the chamber, "but it doesn't say I must keep her."

Another ripple went through the crowd, the buzz of confusion and whispered questions. My heart sank. My mouth went dry. Was this it? He had secured his title and his inheritance, and now he would reject me?

He turned to me and said, "Eldon, take off the shoe."

I did, and the spell fall away. It felt like dropping a heavy wool cloak from my shoulders. I half expected to see some remnant of it puddled on the floor around my feet—one of which was now bare. I looked up to find Xavier smiling at me. "And there's the boy I fell in love with."

"Son," the king said quietly, "I'm not sure this entirely appropriate."

Xavier smiled at me. "Appropriate is boring."

This time, he kissed me the right way, deep and sweet and passionate. There was more cheering, and a celebration that spread throughout the land and lasted a fortnight. And so it was that Augustus Alexandre Kornelius Xavier Redmond became the Crown Prince, and I became both his husband and his wife. More importantly, I remained forevermore his partner, and his friend. He swept me away to his castle where we had fish for dinner once a week, and champagne that tasted like sunlight, and Milton never tired of playing fetch with that silly old shoe.

And the three of us lived—

Well....

I'm sure you can guess how it ends.

About the Author

Marie Sexton lives in Colorado. She's a fan of just about anything that involves muscular young men piling on top of each other. In particular, she loves the Denver Broncos and enjoys going to the games with her husband. Her imaginary friends often tag along. Marie has one daughter, two cats, and one dog, all of whom seem bent on destroying what remains of her sanity. She loves them anyway.

Website and Blog:
http://mariesexton.net/

Facebook:
http://www.facebook.com/MarieSexton.author/

Twitter:
https://twitter.com/MarieSexton

Email:
msexton.author@gmail.com

Also by Marie Sexton:

Promises
A to Z
The Letter Z
Strawberries for Dessert
Paris A to Z
Fear, Hope, and Bread Pudding
Between Sinners and Saints
Song of Oestend
Saviours of Oestend
Second Hand
Never a Hero
Family Man
Flowers for Him
One More Soldier
Cinder: A CinderFella Story
Blind Space
Normal Enough
Roped In
Release by A.M. Sexton
Return by A.M. Sexton
Lost Along the Way
Shotgun
Winter Oranges

Praise for Marie Sexton's

Song of Oestend

1st Place for Best Gay Fantasy in the 2011 Rainbow Awards

"Symbols have power, which Aren and Deacon prove when
death threatens to separate them, but those symbols are
made even more powerful when constructed in love. Though
the journey isn't always easy, though it takes some time for
Aren and Deacon to find the crossroads that will alter the
paths their lives have been on, it was so well worth the trip."

-- Top 2 Bottom Reviews

"Song of Oestend is another fantastic offering from one of
the best writers in this genre."

-- Bittersweet Reviews

Praise for Marie Sexton's

Never a Hero

"If you're all about the character-driven romance? Oh yeah,
Never a Hero is the book for you."

-- The Allure of Books

"The story was brilliantly written, creating a world of
sensitivity and reality through the psyche of both Nick and
Owen." –

- The Jeep Diva

"The writing is great, as you can pretty much count on with
Marie Sexton. I fell in love right along with Owen and Nick.
And while this is book 5 in the Tucker Springs series, it
works 100% as a standalone. I would definitely recommend
this one to m/m romance readers!"

-- Red Hot Books

Praise for Marie Sexton's

Between Sinners and Saints

"I absolutely loved this book and highly recommend it."

-- *Reviews by Jessewave*

"I would strongly recommend Between Sinners and Saints to any fan of the M/M genre and will be reading this story again in the future."

-- *Literary Nymphs Reviews*

"This was an emotional book about trust, love and true devotion. The love scenes were sweet and sensuous and I couldn't get enough of them."

— *Dark Divas Reviews*